SOARING EAGLE

The Santa Fe Trail Trilogy

Young Adult Classics of the American West

by Mary Peace Finley

"Finley's Santa Fe Trail Trilogy…definitely a worthy batch of books for older children."
— SOUTHWEST BOOK VIEWS

SOARING EAGLE
Colorado Authors' League Top Hand Award
Colorado Blue Spruce Finalist
Colorado Book Award Nominee

WHITE GRIZZLY
Benjamin Franklin Award
Colorado Book Award Finalist

MEADOW LARK
Colorado Book Award
WILLA Award Finalist

A Teachers' Guide to Soaring Eagle, written and developed by Sherry Holland and Diane Eussen with drawings by Mary Ann Gabriel, supplements the study of history of the western United States in the mid-1800s. The guide includes classroom aids and activities matched to language arts, social studies, and geography standards and includes a board game based on the events in the book.

A teachers' guide for *White Grizzly* entitled *Novel Talk* was developed by teacher and author Jeanette Haberkorn. This paragraph-by-paragraph literature guide leads students in an in-depth examination of character development, story line, literary elements, and comprehension.

The Santa Fe Trail Trilogy and the
Teachers' Guides are published by Filter Press
www.filterpressbooks.com

SOARING EAGLE

Mary Peace Finley

Book one
The Santa Fe Trail Trilogy

Filter Press, LLC
Palmer Lake, Colorado

To
Ruth, Tim, and Tony
who, like Julio, have
wondered who they are.

Library of Congress Cataloging-in-Publication Data

Finley, Mary Peace.
   Soaring Eagle / Mary Peace Finley.
      p. cm. — (Santa Fe Trail trilogy; bk. 1)
Sequel: White grizzly.
Summary: Julio, a thirteen-year-old boy in 1845, finds friendship and a
clue to his identity while living with the Cheyenne tribe that rescued
him on the Santa Fe Trail.
   ISBN 978-0-86541-096-1 (pbk. : alk. paper)
   [1. Survival—Fiction. 2. Identity—Fiction. 3. Cheyenne Indians—
Fiction. 4. Indians of North America—Great Plains—Fiction. 5.
Hispanic Americans—Fiction. 6. Great Plains—History—19th
century—Fiction.] I. Title.
   PZ7.F4962So 2009
   [Fic]—dc22

                                                    2009003751

Published by Filter Press, LLC, Palmer Lake, Colorado
Cover art copyright © 1993 Ronald Himler
Line drawings copyright © 1998 Mary Ann Gabriel

Printed in the United States of America

Acknowledgments

For all those who assisted with this book, I am grateful. Special thanks to Alexandra Aldred, Bill Gwaltney, and the staff of Bent's Old Fort National Historic Site; historian Dr. David Sandoval; author N. Scott Momaday for reading an early draft of the manuscript and cheering me onward; Kathleen Phillips, Barbara Steiner, Connie Hubbell, Robert Sullivan, John and Bonnie Williams, Jean and Pattie Schnetzler, Claudia Plattner, and Gary Hollenbaugh, O.D., for critiques, information, and nudges; Starr Svaldi and the staff of the Gordon Cooper Public Library in Carbondale, Colorado; George Russ of the Library of Congress; Helen Hooton and Janie Crisp for proofreading; Jane Fitz-Randolph and the members of Prose Pros, mentors of both writers and writing; the Society of Children's Book Writers and Illustrators for education, support, and networks; Wally Finley, my husband, and Ruth Peace, my mother, for their faith and support; Olga Litowinsky, my fine editor; Simon and Schuster for the first five years of *Soaring Eagle* publication, Eakin Press for the second ten years, and Filter Press for the ongoing publication of *Soaring Eagle*, *White Grizzly*, and *Meadow Lark*, the complete Santa Fe Trail Trilogy, young adult literary classics of the American West.

– And for the mystery of the Muses

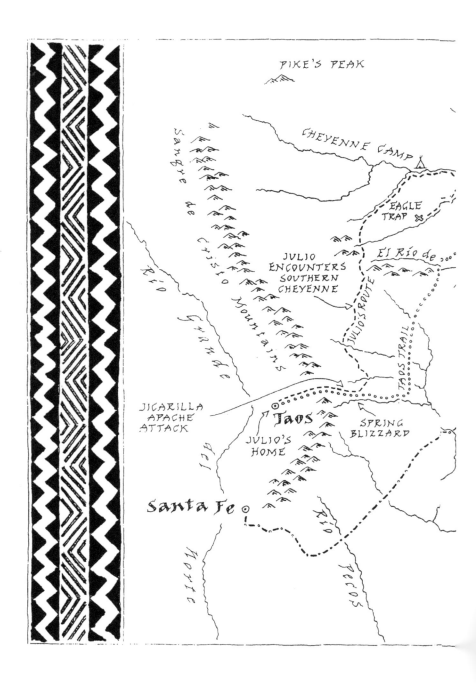

Bent's
Fort

ALTERNATE SANTA FE TRAIL

Arkansas River

las AnimasoPerdidas en Purgatorio

ALTERNATE SANTA FE TRAIL

SANTA FE TRAIL

SANTA FE TRAIL

Bent's
Fort

STATES
of the
UNION

~1845~

Rio Rojo OR Red River

Chapter One

The night was too silent. No sheep bleated, no nighthawk swooped, no cricket chirped.

Julio slipped his reed flute into his bag and scanned the faint outlines of the blue mountains, eyes straining to see through the darkness. He picked up a torch from his small fire and began to circle the flock with Chivita, his sheep dog, at his side.

"Santa María," he prayed aloud, asking for protection from what he felt lurking outside the meadow — wolves, bears, Jicarilla Apaches, spirits...

The sheep grunted and shuffled, averting their eyes from the torch, and tightened into a circle of dusty wool. A newborn lamb bleated. Julio stiffened, listening, senses alert, sliding a tiny silver coin back and forth between his thumb and forefinger. The smells of rich, oily fleece and trampled grass rose to his nostrils. Cool air brushed against his skin. A hoof clicked. Chivita began to growl softly.

Slipping the coin into his bag, Julio dropped the torch. He put a rounded rock in his sling and stood tensed, straining to hear. Still nothing moved in the blackness. Chivita broke into a bark. She raced around the sheep, her black coat swallowed by the night, the white patches flashing like ghosts.

The screams of a terrified lamb and a triumphant yelp— "Yah-hee! Yah!"—shattered the tension.

Julio's sling sliced through the air, spinning the rock toward the voices, but it was too late. The Jicarillas cries and the bleating of the lamb faded up the hillside, swallowed by the night.

"Chivita! Come back," Julio called. "Chivita!"

Panting, Chivita returned, her small muscular body quivering.

"I hate them!" Clenching his teeth, Julio knelt and stroked Chivita's short wiry hair, letting his hand say the anger in his voice was not for her. "They're too lazy to work! They let *us* work, then they steal! We've lost another lamb."

Aching over the loss, Julio reached into the leather bag hanging at his side. His fingers felt the stones ready for the sling, his fire flints and *mechas,* the wicks his sisters had twisted for him from tree cotton to catch sparks, and found what he was searching for his reed flute. Easing down onto the ground, he scratched behind Chivita's ear, then began to play.

The soft music calmed the sheep and him. The harm was done. The Jicarillas would not be back, not tonight. But he wished, as he had every night for three years, he were at Bent's Fort with Papá.

Chapter Two

Morning dawned with a cloudless sky. Sunlight sparkled on the dew. Lying in the meadow Julio felt the warmth touch his hands and face. He swung his legs over the side of his cot of woven leather and spread his damp sarape out to dry. He smiled down at the sparkling white lamb with floppy ears that was tripping over its feet, trying to keep up with its breakfast. "You are fortunate, little one. It wasn't you the Jicarillas carried away for their stew last night."

Bells rang their welcome to the day, echoing up and down the Taos valley. So close to home and Father Martínez and the church, the loss from the raid last night seemed even greater. But, Julio knew, this was the way it had been for the two hundred years the Montoyas had been in the Taos valley—an endless struggle to protect crops and sheep. And themselves.

Julio crossed himself and knelt in the wet grass. Chivita nuzzled his face, but Julio pushed her away. "Not now, Chivita. Now we must pray."

"Padre nuestro…" He had only begun the "Our Father" when the excited voice of his friend José called to him from across the meadow.

"Hey, Green Eyes! Go home! Quick! I'll watch the flock for you. Your Papá has returned!"

"Papá? Papá's home?"

"Julio!" José was staring at him. "What's the matter with you? You've been waiting three years for him. Now what are you waiting for? A burro to give you a ride?"

Already running, Julio swept his sarape from the cot. "Nothing! Chivita! Chivita! Come on! Let's go!"

He and Chivita dashed through the meadows, past fields ready to be planted, to the village of Taos. Chickens fluttered out of their path. Roosters crowed.

Even this early the excitement of a fandango was pulsing in the air. His father had not come alone. Trappers' horses and traders wagons cluttered the plaza. Clumsy wagons held together with strips of rawhide and pegs creaked and yowled along the streets on wooden wheels. Tonight there would be a huge celebration, maybe the biggest of 1845, and Taos, always ready for a party, would be wild.

Julio zigzagged through the dusty lanes past small adobe houses where shawled women leaned against doorposts, smoking their *cigarillos,* chatting with the men from the mountains. He dodged burros eating garbage and a horse laden with an ornate silver saddle with silver stirrups and a bridle whose reins were studded with silver conchas. Someone famous from the capital must also have arrived. Perhaps it was a merchant heading east toward the Santa Fe Trail to trade in the United States, someone who might have taken him along. But now that Papá was home...

He skidded to a stop in front of his family's adobe house. "Papá!" Chivita rushed at Papá's legs, barking.

His whole family was there, Mamá and all eight of his sisters. Gabriela Ultima, the youngest, peeked out from behind her mother's skirts at the father she had never known. Papá was standing in front of them all, as dark and handsome as he had always been. He was still wearing the sheepskin vest he had worn the day he left. The muscles of his arms bulged beneath a clean white shirt, but his shoulders stooped now, like those of a man defeated. His gear was strewn about the yard as if it had been ransacked, and what looked to Julio like a fortune in gold and silver coins sparkled in Mamá's outspread hands.

Papá turned away from his wife and daughters toward Julio. A look of bewilderment and then astonishment passed over his face. The corner of his left eye twitched. For a second he did not move. "Ay, mi hijo!" His words exploded through the tension. "My son!" His voice broke. "You have become a man!" He opened his arms, ignoring

Chivita's tugging at his trousers, and locked Julio into his embrace. Papá's chest, as firm as the adobe bricks he made, pressed hard against Julio and shook as if with laughter, but Julio knew he was not laughing.

"Welcome home, Papá." His words were muffled in the shoulder of the sheepskin vest that smelled of his father, of his tobacco, of places far away. "I've missed you, Papá."

When Julio finally pulled back, tears were stinging his cheeks. Tears were streaming from his father's eyes too. "And I've missed you, my son. Every day I was gone, I thought of you. I prayed for you." Papá tried to knuckle the top of Julio's head, the way he always had, but now he reached up instead of down, and Julio ducked away.

Julio's father wiped his cheeks with the palms of his hands and turned. "I prayed for *all* of you." Papá's eyes swept across the yard toward his wife. His smile faded.

Like the girls' Mamá's face was covered with the red juice of the *alegría* plant to keep the sun from darkening her skin. Tonight she and his sisters would wash off the red, then replace it with white powder made from pounded deer antlers. They would dress in silk and satin with combs and bows in their uncovered hair and flash like bright trumpet flowers at the fandango.

But Julio could tell something was wrong. Mamá held her head high, defiant. Her eyes flashed a warning, daring Julio to speak. He looked back at her in silence, then dropped his gaze. No one not even little Gabriela Ultima, moved.

It was Teresita who broke Mamá's spell. "Please, Papá. We've missed you too. Please don't be angry with Mamá for not wanting you to leave again so soon."

"Pah! Let him rumble like an old bear!" Mamá tossed her head at Teresita. "What do I care if he goes?" She flounced toward the house, scattering daughters and squawking chickens. "Magdalena, María Jesús, Constancia, help me with the cooking! "

She stooped through the low doorway. She was still carrying the coins—enough money, Julio knew, finally to get vigas, the long beams for a bigger house. Tight-lipped and as tense as a bowstring, Julio's father stared after her, squinting. The corner of his left eye twitched violently as if it alone, uncontrolled, could express his rage. Julio had almost forgotten that twitch, how it flickered when Papá was upset, pressing stubby eyelashes against high cheekbones, straight and harsh. Abruptly Julio's father shook a blanket from the dust and rolled it into a tight coil.

"Teresita," Julio whispered, "what happened? Why is Mamá acting that way?" No wonder he preferred the solitary life of the pasture to living at home. "Why are women like that?"

"Julio!" Teresita's palm landed on his cheek. "I'm not!" She backed away, staring at her hand as if it were not her own. Julio was stunned. Papá's frenetic packing stopped.

Gabriela Ultima ran into the house, wailing.

"I'm sorry, Julio," Teresita whispered, touching his face. "But you don't understand." She looked from him to Papá. "With Papá gone, Mamá is lonely."

Their father spun around, snatched a tin cup from the dirt, and flung it into a canvas pouch. "It's a long way to come to be thrown out of my own home. I thought she'd be glad to see me, even for two days."

"Two days!" Julio looked from his father to his sister. "Papá, where are you going now?"

His father sighed and rubbed his hand across his face. "El señor Bent needed someone trustworthy to carry a message to his brother, Charles, here in Taos. I volunteered so I could see you. Now I have a letter to return to Bent's Fort." He touched his chest, and beneath the white cotton Julio heard the crunch of paper. "The United States have elected a new president, a man named Polk. They have admitted Texas into their union, and now there are rumors of war between Mexico and the United States. The Bents are worried."

Papá's gear was repacked. He stood with his load draped across his shoulders and hanging at his sides. The longing in his eyes was so intense as he watched Teresita standing beneath the willows, Julio had to look away. "Take care of yourself, my beautiful daughter," Julio's father said, "and take care of your Mamá and sisters." He turned and walked from the silent yard.

Julio stood, stunned. "But Papá! You said you had two days! Where are you going?"

"Tell your mother..." Papá raised his voice as he glanced toward the shadowy doorway. "Tell your mother and sisters—good-bye for me."

"Papá," Julio called, rushing after him. "Papá, I'm going with you."

Chapter Three

Early the next morning Julio paused outside the small adobe house. Mamá would be groggy from all the dancing and from drinking too much Taos Lightning, but he couldn't bear to leave without say in a final good-bye, free, he hoped, of fighting.

"You want to take him out into that no-man's land," his mother had screamed at Papá last night, "where there is no church, no civilization, only snakes and arrows? You want to take him out there to die? Leave his sisters and me here alone with no man to defend us? It is bad enough that *you* should go again, but to take Julio—he's only a boy!"

It was not until Papá promised they would return before winter that Mamá finally gave in. Still she was not appeased. After the fandango she went to the church.

The *rebozo* covering her hair, her clothing, everything she wore was black, as if someone had died.

Now, as Julio slipped inside the door, his mother's voice whispered. "Julio, your father is a fool! You should not go with him into that ungodly wilderness." He peered in through the stuffy darkness that smelled of the night and stepped to his mother's mat where it was spread on the hard-packed floor. Her hair, gathered into a thick braid, fell like a frayed rope over one shoulder.

"Mamá"—Julio crouched beside her, whispering—"I hoped we could say good-bye without getting angry." Julio knew that after all the fighting last night Papá had come back home. He and Mamá were here, laughing and whispering after everyone had gone to bed. Papá had gotten up early this morning and left.

"I'm not angry!" Mamá's breath smelled of strong corn whiskey. Her voice was gruff, but her face held a hint of tenderness as she reached out to touch his arm. "What's out there in that wilderness? Savages. Texans. Wild animals. I'm afraid, Julio. If you go"—she held him immobile with her eyes—"you will die."

Julio moved out of her grasp. She scooted up against the wall, adjusting the blanket. "I don't want your Papá to go, but he is too proud to listen. Don't let his pride drag you away too."

"It wasn't Papá's idea." Julio spoke calmly, looking directly at her. "I would have gone anyway, Mamá. Before

Papá came back, I had already decided."

"But why? What's so terrible here that makes you want to dance with death in the wilderness? We have enough money for vigas. We can build a new house, a bigger house. You can have a room away from the girls."

"Mamá, there are things I have to know. Only Papá can tell me."

"So it's *that* again." She snorted. "Then you are right about one thing. You will have to ask your father."

She hoisted herself to her feet, adjusted her loose nightgown, then crossed the tiny room, stepping over beds. "But there is no reason, Julio. You are my son, mine as much as his!" Julio watched her lumber past his mat, which was rolled up against the wall to save space and to be used as a chair during the day. In the middle of the dirt floor lay the striped rough-spun rug of red and green and yellow, Mamá's pride. He remembered the day she had finished making it.

"Here," she whispered, "take this." From the small family altar in the corner, she removed a carved wooden statue and kissed it. "Keep it with you always, Julio. It is Saint Christopher, the patron saint of those who journey. Pray to him. He will guard over you and protect you." She shoved the small figure into his hands, then turned. "Come."

He followed her to another corner, where dried herbs hung from the vigas that supported the roof. Little clay pots sat on rough wooden shelves along the wall. "Take this also," she said, handing him one of the pots. "It is tallow. Add this." She crushed leaves from two of the dried boughs, then reached into a leather bag, mixed another powdered herb with them, and brushed the whole mixture into the pot. "It is medicine—osha, contrayerba, and flowers of chamomile. Heat it with the candle, then soak a rag in the mixture to put on cuts or sores."

"Gracias, Mamá, but please, don't worry. I'll be all right."

"All right!" she mimicked, her voice out of control, waking the girls. "Nobody—not el señor St. Vrain, not el señor Bent or his brothers, not even Kit Carson—goes on that Taos Trail, up over Raton Pass, alone! Nobody but your fool Papá! Doesn't he know you could be killed? Don't *you*? Why won't you wait until a caravan is going so you won't be alone? *Ay!*"

Sleepy-eyed, his sisters cowered silently in their beds, listening, watching. Chivita whimpered outside.

"Mamá, please, don't cry. Yesterday Papá met some traders with wagons. That's why we have to go now, to travel with them. Please, Mamá, we'll be all right. Just last night"—he was speaking to his sisters as much as to Mamá—"as I was praying to the Virgin, I had a wonderful feeling. I've never felt that way before. It was as if she were telling me, Yes! You should go."

His mother looked at him for a long while, gazing so deeply into his eyes, Julio wanted to bolt and run. Finally, crossing herself, she said, "You were almost my son, Julio, my only son. Vaya con Dios—go with God." She wrapped her arms around him, pulling him close, then released him. Sniffing, she shuffled out the back door.

Around the room the quiet crying of his sisters tugged at him, making him want to run, making him want to stay. He lifted Gabriela Ultima and brushed away her tears. "Don't cry, Gabrielita. I'll bring you a present when I come back," he said, nuzzling her with his nose. "Would you like that?"

Gabriela Ultima, damp from the night's sleep, tucked her ear to her shoulder and sniffed. Pouting, she said, "What?"

"Something you've never seen before; something I've never seen either. Something from the new place where I'm going."

"For me too?" It was Rosita.

"And you."

"And me?" Alicia asked.

"And you. And you and you and you and you and you!" Setting Gabriela Ultima back on her bed, he promised them all, touching each one on the head, like a priest bestowing blessings. Then he grabbed up his bag, a drinking gourd, his sarape and sombrero, and a canvas bag of meat scraps for Chivita and dashed away from the place which had been home for as long as he could remember, wondering when, if ever, he would return.

"Wait! Julio, wait!" Running barefooted, her long black hair flying, nightclothes flapping around her legs, Teresita caught up with him. She faced him, her white sleeping shift rising and falling with each heavy breath. "Julio, please tell me. I know what you told everyone at the fandango—that you want to make adobes at Bent's Fort, that you want to go with Papá. But that's not all, is it? Julio?" she whispered. Her eyes, soft and deep, filled with a mixture of awe and compassion. "It's what we've talked about before, isn't it? The green eyes..."

Julio nodded. "I can't keep anything hidden from you, can I?" Teresita looked down, her black eyelashes fanning, like Papá's, against the same bronzed skin. "But I do want to work at Bent's Fort. Make adobes there. I've always wanted to. Even if Papá hadn't come back, I would have gone—soon."

Teresita's eyes darted back toward the house. "Yes!" she whispered. "I'd go too if I were you. And I will when I have a chance. I want to see what's over those mountains. I want to see everything! Do everything!" She spun in a circle, hands held high over her head.

"Teresita, you worry me. I watched you last night. I saw the way you flirted with the foreigners at the fandango, the way those men followed you with their eyes. It scares me, the way you think."

"Julio, I'm thirteen years old! Old enough to get married, but I can't even run off to the fields to be alone with my dreams the way you can. You're not the only one with dreams! I'm not going to live cramped in a little adobe hut for the rest of my life!" She gestured at the chicken-fouled dirt yard. "How else can I escape from this except to find a man?"

"I thought you liked José."

"José! José will stay in Taos forever." Teresita spun away from him and ran toward the willow-lined stream near the house. It was Teresita's favorite place, where the two of them had played away their childhood.

"Teresita?" Julio crawled into their alcove of green leaves and sat beside her.

"Julio—" She lowered her eyes and clutched her arms around her knees. "I'm sorry about yesterday. I'm sorry I slapped you. It's just—I don't want to be like Mamá."

For a while there was only the kind of silence that speaks when words fail.

"Yesterday after you and Papá left, I asked Mamá again if you had another mother."

Julio flinched. "What did she say this time?"

"She said, 'No! Of course not!' So I asked her, 'But what about his eyes? The rest of us don't have green eyes, or such light skin. Or hair the color of straw. And he's so tall. He doesn't look like any of us.' 'Well!' Mamá said." Teresita imitated her perfectly. "She gave me that look, stuck her head up high and raised her eyebrows. 'I suppose his father *might* have been American,' she said, and then she got weepy again and started ranting about Papá stealing away her only son." Teresita shook her head. "Maybe she doesn't know."

"But if *she* doesn't know, who does? I've asked Father Martínez and Uncle Rumaldo, I've asked the old widow, I've asked everyone!"

"I hope you find out, Julio. I hope Papá can tell you— *will* tell you." Teresita pressed something round and hard into the palm of his hand. "I want to give this to you. It's a stone—a magic stone. I found it in the sand over there by the river when we were little. I've kept it with me always. Whenever I've been sad or lonely, or afraid for us or Papá, I've held it for luck. Take it with you." She looked down, then added so softly Julio could barely hear, "When you hold it, will you remember...?" She bit her lip. Her eyes were misting.

"Of course, I'll remember you! But we'll see each other again." Julio's voice pushed past the lump in his throat. "And when we do, I'll give back your stone, and you'll give *this* back to me." He reached into his bag. Balancing the tiny silver coin on the tip of his finger, he dropped it into the palm of her hand.

"You can't give me this!" she exclaimed. "Papá gave it to you. You've had it forever!"

"It's not a gift, just a trade, remember? Until we see each other again. All right?"

Teresita closed her fingers around the tiny coin. "All right. And then you can tell me what you've learned." Her voice stretched between tears and a smile. "And what's out there beyond those mountains."

"I promise."

"May God protect you, Julio."

"And you, my sister," Julio said. "¡Adiós!"

Chapter Four

The central plaza of Taos was deserted at that early hour. Julio's father was tying a leather thong under the belly of a small gray-brown burro loaded with a pack. Chivita ran ahead, sniffing circles.

"Where did you get him?" Julio slowed his pace, not to spook the little donkey. His hand slid over the prickly hair on the nose and up the soft, warm ears. Horses would have been better, but only the rich owned horses, and Julio had never learned to ride. A burro, though, would make the nearly two-hundred mile journey much easier. Perhaps with what was in the pack he and Papá would not have to hunt for all their food.

"Good morning!" Papá grunted as he tightened a strap. "I look at you, I still can't believe what I see." He shook his head. "When I left, I had a boy. Now I look into the eyes of a young man." He tightened his fist into a ridge of knuckles, but, laughing, Julio jerked his chin upward and dodged.

"That worked better when I was short, Papá."

"Yes, well—" Papá patted the donkey. "El señor St. Vrain asked us to deliver Romeo to el señor William Bent at Bent's Fort." Romeo twisted his long ears as if he recognized his name. "He is a good man, el señor St. Vrain, a good Catholic."

Julio admired the load. A shiny new tin coffee pot hung next to the drinking gourds. Coffee. He could almost smell it boiling on the campfire. "Let's get going!" he said. "What are we waiting for?"

His father chuckled. "So you're ready, are you?"

"Yes!"

"It won't be an easy trip."

"I know."

"We'll follow the Taos Trail east along Rayado Creek, then go north to the Arkansas River. It could be dangerous." The corner of his father's left eye twitched.

"You've made the trip without trouble. Twice."

"Four times. Not always without trouble. Once we came close to being attacked by the Arapaho." Papá was checking him over as if he were still a child. He lifted the corner of his sarape and inspected the knife hanging from the red sash at his waist, his leather bag, and freshly washed white pants and shirt. "You should have boots."

Julio glanced down at the sandals on his feet. "These are all I have."

His father shrugged. "Your feet won't like the cactus," he said and gave the burro a tug.

"Vamos, Chivita!" Uncle Rumaldo had tried to keep Chivita as a part of the bargain for taking care of the sheep while they were gone. Everyone knew she was the best sheep dog in the Taos valley, especially Uncle Rumaldo. Papá had taken her, newborn, and suckled her on a nanny goat so she would learn to be gentle. That was why Julio had named her Chivita, "Little Goat."

"But Uncle Rumaldo didn't get you, did he, Little Goat?"

Julio slapped her on the rump, then broke into a run. "To the mountains! To the desert! To William Bent's fort on the Arkansas River!" They were on their way.

Soon they were leaving the green valley of Taos, following the mountain trail upward. Piñon, juniper, and sage grew along the way, and as Julio and his father climbed higher, the shadows of pine, scrub oak, and spruce crossed the trail. Bright yellow glacier lilies pushed up through the edges of melting snowbanks. Julio plucked a fuzzy catkin from a quaking aspen tree—a first bud of spring—and rubbed it against his cheek.

Within hours they had gone a greater distance from home than Julio had been before. He could not remember ever being so far away from other people. Chivita dashed in and out of trees, nosing under bushes, disappearing into the forest, only to return, panting, to do it all again.

The sun moved overhead, and as it sank low in the afternoon sky behind them, his father began to sing softly in a low, mournful tone. Julio slowed to listen.

"For I'm going away
And I don't know if I'll return.
Memories of an ungrateful woman
I'll carry in my soul.
If by chance, on the road
I'm shot down by my enemies,
With my last sigh
I'll send word
So you will know."

Julio wished he could do something to make his father feel better, but few words had been spoken all day, and he didn't know how to begin. Mamá did care about Papá, he was sure, but she was too proud to show it, or to say she was sorry. Or maybe Papá was too proud to accept her apology. It was confusing, complicated. "I'll never get married!" Julio promised himself. He was startled by Papá's curt laugh. He had spoken aloud.

During the second day his father's spirits seemed to rise, especially when they reached the first pass. Coming

down was much easier than the upward climb had been—
they had been pushing as hard as they could to catch up
with the lumbering wagons. Maybe this would be the day
he and Papá could talk.

The trail wound out from a grove of tall aspens onto an
overlook with a panoramic view. Below lay a forest that
sloped down to the foot of the mountain, and beyond it lay
another valley with a broad meadow that made it almost a
twin to the valley of Taos.

"Look at the eagle." Julio pointed toward a bird circling
gracefully over the valley. "I feel like that." He smiled at
Papá. It was as if nothing had changed between them in
those lonely three years. "There should be two of them.
One for me. One for you."

"The Cheyenne at the fort would say it is a good omen."
His father rubbed Romeo's muzzle and let the reins drop.
"Have you been watching the trail?"

Julio nodded. He had been studying the wagon tracks
all day, wondering when he and his father would catch
up to the traders. The marks in the dirt were not old. His
father scanned the expanse below, shading his eyes. The
twitch in his left eye returned.

Like a jewel, a stream broke out of the forest and
glistened through the vast meadow, and in the distance a
small lake shone in the sun. Across the meadow the path
seemed to narrow into a single line that vanished into the
tall pines on the other side of the valley. Julio could not

see the wagons. His muscles tensed.

"Could they have crossed already?" His fingers felt for Teresita's white stone.

"It's possible."

But Julio knew from the tone of Papá's voice it was equally possible they had not. If the wagons were hidden in the thickly wooded slope between here and the meadow, he and Papá should hurry. That way they would not have to travel the meadow alone.

"This way," his father said. He took Romeo's rope and led him off the trail. "We'll leave the path and make camp for the night."

It was too early. The sun had only begun to move downward. "Come, Chivita," Julio whispered, edging between aspen and pine. "Keep quiet." For the first time he believed the only thing that his parents had agreed upon: *This journey could be dangerous.*

Deep in the forest off the trail they found the stream. His father chose a place, but he did not begin to gather wood for a fire.

"Tomorrow," his father whispered, "we will look out again across the valley. If we see the wagons, then we will know. Tonight we'll be safer here."

Later, when the sun began to set, they were hungry. Dinner was *atole*, dried corn his mother and sisters had roasted and ground on the stone metate. Julio and his father mixed the atole with cold water from the stream and ate it.

When their stomachs were full, they leaned back against the tree trunks, huddled under their sarapes, and Chivita laid her head in Julio's lap. Papá rolled his strong tobacco in corn shucks. From his leather bag Julio drew out the new mecha Teresita had made. He removed the copper tube from the end, struck his flint to the steel, caught a spark on the cotton, then lit his father's cigarillo.

It seemed to Julio that the oncoming darkness was charged with unseen spirits, as on the nights when he knew there was something threatening his sheep. He wondered if something had happened to the wagons, then accused his imagination of playing tricks on him, making him afraid of the dark like a child. He found Teresita's stone, fingered it, and said a prayer to Saint Christopher for protection.

"Julio—" Papá's voice was a coarse whisper.

Chivita raised her head, then lowered it again.

"Yes, Papá?"

"I'm glad you came with me, Julio. It's time for you to live in the world of men, in your own world." His father's cigarillo glowed in the half-light of evening. He began to talk, the soft rhythm of his voice blending with the rustle of aspen leaves and the rushing of the stream. "Julio, remember what I told you before we left? I was nearly attacked by the Arapaho? When I was young like you, thirteen, fourteen years old, I..."

Julio sat in silence, waiting, listening not only to the

story but also to the sounds of the forest. An owl hooted nearby. He crossed himself and hugged Chivita to his chest.

"When summer came," his father continued, "my *compañeros* and I were heading back to Taos along the branch of the Santa Fe Trail that crosses the Purgatory."

"Purgatory!" Julio whispered.

"It's a stream. El Río de las Animas Perdidas en Purgatorio—the River of Lost Souls in Purgatory." Julio shifted uneasily. "A long time ago—two hundred years, maybe more—Spanish explorers were searching for Quivira, Coronado's lost cities of gold. They had orders to return to Mexico City, but they refused, so their priest left without blessing their mission. They were all killed. Years later explorers found what was left—rusted armor and arrows and pieces of bone. That's where the name came from; it was called the River of Souls Lost in Purgatory because they died without a priest's blessing."

Goosebumps rose on the back of Julio's neck. That was a story to be told in the light of day, not alone on a forbidding trail in the dark. But Papá was in a storytelling mood.

"Anyway, as I was saying, we were heading back to Taos along the branch of the Santa Fe Trail that crosses the Purgatory. We were up on a bluff above the trail. We'd had a long morning, then ate too much fresh antelope. It was a blistering hot July afternoon, and we all fell asleep in the cedars. Arapaho war cries woke us. We thought we were dead for sure. We grabbed our guns and jumped up, but the attack was below us on the trail. We crawled to the edge of the bluff and looked down."

Chivita raised her head. Her ears pointed toward the dark trees. "Papá, can't we talk about something else?" Julio whispered.

"Let me finish, Son. This is important to you. It's where your silver coin came from." Papá's hand reached out and rested on Julio's knee. "They were far south for Arapaho, but that's what they were. After they rode off, shouting and waving their prizes, we crept down to the wagon." He shook his head. "I suppose nobody'll ever know how that wagon got to be out there all by itself. It was standing where it stopped, looking like nothing had happened, but inside, both the man and the woman were dead. A little girl too."

"Why are you telling me this?" Julio couldn't stand any more. "Arapahos are as bad as Apaches! The Apaches come down from the mountains to kill and steal. Arapahos do this! They're savages! All of them! I'm going for a drink of water."

Julio sprang to his feet, throwing aside his sarape and sombrero. Chivita leapt aside, growling low. There was still enough light to see his way to the stream.

"They're not all bad." His father's voice rose to a half whisper behind him. "What about the people in the Taos Pueblo? The Cheyenne at Bent's Fort? From what I've seen, there are good people and bad people in every nation. Julio, there's someone at the fort now who may know who the people in the wagon were. There was a little boy, too, a baby—"

As Papá's voice droned on, Julio knelt and bent toward the ice-cold water. He reached down with his gourd. Over the sound of the stream Papá's tale continued. "...skinny little thing, bundled in a blanket in that blazing July heat." He chuckled. "Real cute..."

"...why..." Behind him a sound sliced through the air. "...name..." Chivita snarled. "...is —Julio! Get down!" Papá shouted. As if his father's story had conjured them up, figures leapt from behind the trees and were everywhere. Apaches!

Julio froze. His eyes searched frantically for a place to hide. Nothing! Nothing but the bank of the stream. He flattened himself to the ground and rolled into the water. Inching noiselessly under the embankment, he grabbed on to the naked roots that trailed down into the stream.

The water was freezing, so cold that at first it felt as if it were burning him. Pulling himself up with the roots, he wedged his body against the bank out of the current, then strained to hear. From above, Romeo's frightened brays mixed with the cries of the warriors. They were calling to one another, trying to find him, Julio was certain. Chivita's wild barking broke into a long high-pitched scream and then into a series of yelps that faded away.

Frenzied thoughts swirled through his brain. *Chivita, hide with Papá! Papá, you're hiding, too, in the trees. That's why I don't hear your voice. Ay, Santa María, Mother of God, help him! Help us all. Mamá! You were right—we shouldn't have come alone. Teresita—*His fingers yearned to touch her magic stone. The muscles in his arms burned from supporting his weight. His feet and lower legs, splashed by the stream, were growing numb.

Papá, we have only to keep quiet until they go away. Then we will find each other again. Like the Hail Marys of the rosary, his thoughts repeated over and over. *We will find each other. Find each other. Find each other. Ay, Dios!* It was all he could do to keep from crying aloud. *When will they leave?*

The sounds of searchers still came from overhead Romeo continued to bray but not as frantically as before. He couldn't hear Chivita at all.

Finally there was nothing but silence and darkness, and the cold of death creeping up his legs into his body. But he would not move. *They're waiting for us, Papá. Keep still! They haven't gone. It's a trick.*

He listened for Romeo but heard nothing. *They've taken Romeo away so I won't hear him, but they're still waiting for me. I'll freeze in this stream before I let them capture me.*

Shivers racked him. His hands held on with the grip of death, impossible to open. The cold ceased to be cold, and his mind drifted into another place, far away, a place of light where the delicate scent of lilies of the valley filled the air.

"Bill-y...Bill-y..." The music of a woman's voice was calling to him. It was to him though it was not his name. "Billy..." A song floating on air. "It's not time yet, Billy. Wake up. Wake up and dry yourself. The danger has passed."

Julio struggled against the blackness in his mind. He did not want to wake up.

"Billy!" The voice was stronger now. A command.

What? Where was he? Cold. So cold. He forced open his eyes, facing mud.

"Gracias, Santa María! Gracias!" To the lady in his vision he gave thanks.

He forced his fingers to straighten, painfully releasing the roots. He fell backward into the water, then staggered and pulled himself up over the embankment onto dry ground. His legs would not hold him. He could not crawl. Starlight cast only hints of light through the darkness, but just before he collapsed, he saw Papá.

Chapter Five

Sunlight filtered down through the trees, warming Julio back to life. His clothes were wet, his skin cold, clammy, pressed into the sharp rocks where he had fallen.

Whatever had touched him before touched him again — a cold nose against his neck. Something sharp tugged and ripped at his leg.

"Chivita!" he cried, rising up. "You made it!" Blinking to clear his vision, he focused, not on Chivita but on bristling silver fur and bared teeth. His hand closed around a stone. With all the strength he had left he jumped to his feet, staggered, almost fell, then whirled dizzily and came face to face with wolves.

Startled, the wolves backed away. It was then Julio saw the rest of the pack.

His scream echoed through the forest. "Papá, no! No! No!" Like a wild animal, he charged them, yelling, "Get away! Get away from him! Get away!" One of the wolves held its ground. Julio grabbed a stick and brought it down hard. The wolf yelped and turned tail.

The rest of the pack slunk away and stood watching, waiting—a momentary reprieve. Moving cautiously, ignoring the pain in his leg, never taking his eyes off the wolves, Julio reached into the leather bag he had hung from the tree the night before. His fingers worked out the sling and a few rocks. One-handed, he loaded the sling. Then, so quickly the wolves had no time to react, he let the first, then the second, then the third rock fly. Yipping in pain, three wolves fled into the woods. The others followed.

Panting, shaking from fatigue, Julio slumped against the trunk of an aspen. His leg hurt. Warm blood trickled into his sandal.

"Chivita? Here, Chivita! Come back now."

He limped to the stream and washed the wound. Later he would use some of Mamá's medicine.

He forced himself to look at Papá. An arrow had ripped through Papá's sarape. His scalp had been taken, and his face was covered with blood. And the wolves had bitten his hands and legs.

"I should never have left you!" Bile welled up inside Julio's throat, and he doubled over with dry heaves. No man should die like this. For the first time in his life Julio knew the meaning of blood lust. Revenge. If he could, he would kill them all. All the wolves. All the savages. Without mercy.

He grabbed his leather bag, felt in it for the statue of Saint Christopher, and clenched the carved figure, strangling it in his fist. "If you are the saint of travelers"—he spat out the words—"if you are to protect us on our journey, then why? Why?" He flung the statue into the dirt. "Oh, Papá! Papá! I wanted to be with you! I wanted you to be happy again! I wanted to know...If only I had stayed with you, together we could have fought them! You'd still be alive!"

No, I'd be dead.

The thought dried his tears. Forcing himself to be calm, to think, he murmured, "Papá, I won't let you be another soul lost in purgatory. I'll find a priest for you! I promise, you'll be buried with a priest's blessing." Julio wiped the salt and mucus from his face. "But until then I'll do the best I can, Papá." Leaning over, he placed the statue of Saint Christopher on his father's chest near the arrow. "He *will* be with you on *this* journey."

Julio staggered to his feet to look for something he could use as a shovel. He followed the Apaches' tracks through the woods, where they had led Romeo away, his eyes scanning the ground. "Chivita? Chivita?" he called. There was no sign of her anywhere.

He found his sarape where he had thrown it, and close by he caught the glint of something shiny in the underbrush—Papá's new coffee pot, used only twice. It must have fallen out of Romeo's pack unnoticed. It would have to do.

He chose a clearing near the stream and started to scrape at the dirt with the coffee pot. The soil blurred as again and again his eyes teared up. Only three days. Three days ago he and Papá had been in Taos, making plans, fighting with Mamá— Now Papá was gone. Now he would never have the chance to work at his side. Now he could never ask him everything he wanted to know.

New questions began to push at him. *Since there is no priest, what will happen to Papá's soul? Will he be like those Spanish soldiers, lost in purgatory? Should I bring Father Martínez from Taos? Should I go home to tell Mamá and my sisters, or should I try to catch up with the wagons? What if the Apaches come back? I can't stay here alone.*

"Chivita! Chivita!"

By the time the sun had passed the highest point in the spring sky, Julio's throat was raw from calling. His fingers were scraped and bleeding, but he had scooped out a shallow grave. A proper grave would take days to dig this way. Papá's body would have to be buried before night and the grave covered with stones. He would not have the strength to fight off wolves another time.

Julio looked down at his father and at the arrow. "You won't need your sarape and vest anymore, will you, Papá? You'd want me to use them, wouldn't you? Everything else is gone." Cringing, he reached for the arrow. "I know this won't hurt you. Not now. But I don't want to do it!" He averted his eyes and jerked the arrow out. With it came a piece of blood-soaked paper. Julio reached inside the shirt and pulled out the rest. It was the letter for Mr. Bent, folded and sealed with wax. He stuck it into his leather bag, then pulled off Papá's sarape, his sheepskin vest, and his leather boots.

Julio knelt once again beside his father. He made the sign of the cross over his chest, slipped the statue of Saint Christopher beneath his father's hands, then crossed himself again. "Our Father, Dios, Jesucristo, Son of God, Santa María, Mother of God—" He blinked, fighting for control. "This is my father. He is—he was—a good man. I will ask for a priest's blessing soon." Then after a long silence he said, "Amen."

He took Papá's feet and dragged the body to the shallow grave. "Adios, Papá," he whispered. "I will miss you."

When the loose dirt was back in the hole, he began to carry rocks. Without them the wolves would dig. Julio shuttled stones from the creek bed until the sun was sinking low in the afternoon and he was too exhausted to carry even one more. Papá's grave was well protected.

There was nothing more he could do for his father—
unless—An idea began to take form.

With his knife he cut two young aspen trees. In the
soft white wood he carved a cross and the year, 1845. He
and José had learned to make numbers from Baldimiro,
the shopkeeper, but he had never learned to read or
write. He could not make Papá's name; he didn't know
how. He placed one aspen across the other, laced them
together with strips of willow bark, and stuck the longest
pole into the ground at the head of the grave, securing it
with stones. As he stood back, the impulse that had been
pushing at him flew through his brain. *Nothing more I can
do—unless I become a priest. Then Papá's burial would
be sanctified. His soul would be free.*

Gathering up the two sarapes, Papá's boots, his leather
bag, and the coffee pot, Julio took one last look back.
"Chivita. Chivita! Come here, Little Goat. Come on."

He retraced his path to the trail. There he took out his
knife and carved in the trunk of a large aspen an arrow
pointing toward the grave—a marker for a world in which
he was alone.

The sun cast shadows from the west. Julio looked back
toward home. Mamá should know what had happened.
Father Martínez could tell him what to do, but the priest at
Bent's Fort could tell him too. He gazed ahead toward the
invisible wagons, toward a journey of many days with no

food or supplies to a place he'd only heard of. He thought of the letter in his bag, and what Papá had said about war. Like a mighty tree in the forest, Julio stood rooted to the trail, unable to move. He was tormented by a question with no right answer.

Chapter Six

Blackbirds chattered in the branches arching over the trail. A robin hopped along the ground, pausing, cocking its head, chirping. A small animal scurried in the undergrowth.

It made no sense to continue. Everything Mamá feared had already happened, except for his being killed. It would be insane to go on.

Papá's song, Papá's voice, echoed in his memory, stirring grief with doubts:

> *"...If, by chance, on the road*
> *I'm shot down..."*

Had Papá known? Had he sensed his death was near?

Finally Julio turned to retrace the two pairs of footprints in the dust.

"...I'll send word
So you will know."

"Chivi—" His voice gave out.

When it became too dark to walk any farther, Julio found a place to rest near the trail. Pain throbbed up his leg, but it seemed separate from him. He was numb. He had not had food all day, but he was not hungry. Papá was dead. Why should he eat?

He had no feeling of being watched or of being followed. He trusted that feeling.

From his bag Julio took out Mamá's herbs and candle. Teresita's mechas caught sparks from his flint stones. He placed the candle against the smoldering cotton and blew. The candle flame leapt to life. He heated the little clay pot, stirring the herbs and tallow with a stick, then tore a strip of cloth from his shirt, dipped it in the solution, and wrapped his leg. The ragged wolf bite had become red and swollen, and the poultice was soothing. *Gracias, Mamá*, he thought. *You don't know Papá is dead. When I tell you—will you care? Or will you only be angry?*

When he replaced the clay pot in his leather bag, his fingers touched something round, and he pulled out Teresita's magic stone. He had almost forgotten it. Lucky he hadn't shot it at the wolves. Poor Teresita. She, yes, would mourn. The image of the two of them—Teresita and Papá—standing together in the yard seemed long ago. He rubbed the white stone, then slipped it back into his leather bag.

He longed for his bed in the pasture and for the familiar solace of the sheep. It would be good to return. It would be the same as before—Papá away, he could pretend, still at Bent's Fort.

Julio raked dry leaves into a hollow between two logs and spread Papá's sarape over them. Before he lay down, he would perform the ritual he and Chivita had done every night, even though he had no torch and no flock, and Chivita was—he couldn't think about what might have happened to Chivita. Biting his lips, clamping his eyelids against the heat rising in his eyes, he began. He picked up a stick, held it as if it were a torch, and slowly walked a circle around his leafy bed, silently asking protection for himself during the night. Without Chivita it seemed hollow, a song without music. He made the sign of the cross, then lay down inside the circle and covered himself with his sarape.

"Santa María, Mother of God," he prayed to the voice that had called to him as he'd clung beneath the stream bank, "care for my father's spirit on his journey. Keep him safe from the evil places. And watch over my mother and sisters at home." His throat began to close again, and he clenched his teeth against the rising tears. "And if my dog, Chivita, is still alive, please...Please send her back to me. Amen."

When he closed his eyes, pictures of Papá's bloodied head flashed in front of him, then wolves and Apaches. His throat was dry. His leg throbbed. In the darkness he thrashed on the cold leaves until, exhausted, he fell asleep.

When he awoke, it was morning. "Chivita?" He looked from side to side, but he was alone. His decision of yesterday was wrong. Now he knew he must go on to Bent's Fort. It was what he'd wanted, and what Papá wanted for him. And he had the letter entrusted to Papá.

Julio treated his wound again, then pulled on Papá's boots. They were too small, and the top rubbed against the wolf bite. He changed back to his sandals, thinking he'd leave the boots behind, but remembered Papá's warning about cactus and decided to take them, at least for now.

He mixed water from his gourd with what was left of the atole in his bag and ate, ignoring the pain caused by the rough corn scratching down his throat. He would have to eat to keep his strength. He would have to walk fast to make up for the day lost. By tonight, he hoped, he would catch up with the wagons. Then he would hunt meat.

Julio tied the extra sarape, Papá's boots and vest, and the coffee pot to the red sash at his waist so he could travel with his hands free and returned to the trail. The uneven rhythm of his pace drummed up that haunting tune, pushing unwanted words through his mind.

"For I'm going away
And I don't know if I'll return.
Memories…"

Julio paused at the tree where he'd carved the arrow. "This is what you would have me do, isn't it, Papá?" he said. "Fly on for both of us, like the eagle." He kneeled and crossed himself. After he prayed, he rose and called for Chivita one last time before he continued on.

When he reached the overlook where he and Papá had stopped before, he gazed once again over the expanse below. As before, no wagons were in sight. If they had crossed the valley yesterday or earlier today, he might still catch up with them.

The trail wound downward, marked with wagon tracks. Julio's taut leg muscles loosened with walking, and he found his usual pace returning. Soon he was at the edge of the meadow. Jittery, he listened, studying the trail, the tracks, and the hills on the far side, where the trail climbed upward again. *The wagons must already have started the long pull up that far slope*, he thought. *That will slow them down, and I can go fast.* If only Papá had kept going…

He loaded his sling, then strode out from the cover of the trees. The peaks of the mountains still wore caps of snow, but the meadow was a lush green dotted with the tiny purple flowers Teresita called stink flowers. The stream, wider here than on the mountain, gurgled past, and Julio scanned the ground, alert for signs of Apaches. Except for the wagon tracks, an occasional boot print, and the droppings of horses, the world seemed deserted.

Julio dropped to his knees beside the stream. Swaying beneath the water were plants he recognized. Cress, green and delicious. With his knife he sliced below the surface. When he had a handful, he swished it in the stream, then ate as he continued his solitary march. Strange, he thought, that his body should crave food even with Papá dead. Life going on, like the wagons there ahead, going on, not knowing what had happened so close behind.

Billowy white clouds, like the clouds of a summer thunderstorm, began to build up behind the mountains. The air became cooler. Julio's brisk pace kept him warm. He ignored the pain in his leg, anxious for a fire and companionship by nightfall. He did not want to spend another night alone, haunted by memories.

Before long the sky turned from fluffy white against blue to gray and black. Distant rain streaked chalky rays on the blackened sky. Mountaintops disappeared under the storm. Wind sliced through the openings of Julio's sarape and threatened to send his sombrero flying.

He tucked the hat into his sash and pushed on. As the temperature dropped, the first flakes appeared, fat moist snowflakes swirling into his face. He clutched the extra sarape over his head, wearing it like a shawl, and blew the tickling snow from his nose. The ruts from the wagon wheels were covering over with white.

The snow became a blizzard, a spring storm unlike storms at any other time of the year. Julio knew such blizzards could come and go in a day with spring on either side, and people would die in their severity. He had to catch up with the wagons, now! Panicked, he ran along the ruts. Instead of pressed earth the wagon tracks soon became raised white lines, then solid white trenches. Snow wedged in the open toes of his sandals. He stamped it out, but within two or three strides the sandals were packed full of snow again. His feet were getting icy. His throat, already raw, was worse.

Not wanting to stop to change to Papá's boots, he pushed on, running, stumbling as the snow fell harder. The wind let up, and the heavy wet snow came down even more thickly, piling higher and higher, covering everything.

Julio darted this way and that, chasing hints of straight lines under the snow. It was useless. The trail was covered.

Sides aching, he unknotted Papá's boots from his sash and stopped long enough to trade sandals for boots. He had to get out of the open and find shelter soon.

Everything looked the same—nothing but dizzying whiteness. Praying he was not walking in circles, Julio set a steady pace, limping as fast as he could toward what he hoped was the opposite side of the valley.

Chapter Seven

Julio had never seen it snow so hard or so fast. In little time the snow had begun to build up on the ground, and now it tumbled over his feet with each step. It blew into his face and clung to his eyelashes and hair. Still he pressed on, gulping cold air down his sore throat, bitter memories swept aside by the struggle.

Something loomed ahead in the swirling white, then disappeared. Julio snatched the knife from his sash. He would have little strength for a battle, but the gnawing hunger in his belly made him hope for game. The swirling snow paused momentarily, and he saw it again. Not game. A tree. And beyond, another tree. "I made it!" His voice was barely a croak. The icy edge of panic melted.

The ground began to rise quickly. He had no idea now where the path was, but peering through the whirling whiteness, he saw what he hoped was a bluff where he might find shelter. Shivering, then sweating, flaming hot, then freezing cold, he struggled to pull dead branches from the pine and spruce trees, making his way toward the shadow. The mountain buffered the wind; the snowfall slackened.

Above him a crevice darkened the rock, and he climbed toward it. It was a hollow place, not as sheltered as a cave but almost as good. He shoved the branches onto the shelf above his head, then worked his way up. The wind did not reach here. Shivering, his hands stiff from cold, Julio laid a fire. He would keep it burning all night. Once he warmed up, he would not want to wade out into the snow again. Reluctantly he gathered more wood and began to make a temporary home in the crevice. *Home.* The word caused a flood of yearning. *Mamá. Teresita. Gabrielita. Chivita. Papá.*

Beneath the wraps his clothes had stayed fairly dry. The rough-spun wool of the sarape had absorbed very little moisture and, even though damp, would keep him warm. But in spite of Papá's boots his feet were painfully cold. He tried to remember what he'd heard about frostbite. The air, in spite of the snow, was mild. He would not freeze to death, but he was worried. He was getting sick, really sick.

Julio huddled next to the small flame, melting snow in the coffee pot, easing hot water down his throat, shivering, sweltering, throwing aside his cover, grasping it to him again. His teeth chattered. His body shook. He almost forgot about the bite on his leg.

He drifted into and out of the fever, rousing to add wood to the fire, slumping again into a fitful sleep. He lost track of time. It was light, then dark.

One time he awoke, blinding sunlight was reflecting off snow and he was crying out "Mamá!" And the next the sky looked as if it were dropping flames on the earth.

"*Chi! Chiti-chit-chiti!*" A chipmunk was perched on the rock above him, scolding. Julio opened his eyes. It was day. Teresita's stone was clenched in his fist.

"Santa María," he prayed. "Gracias a Dios, I am better. Thank you."

The chipmunk scurried out of sight, then peeked back around a rock at Julio, scolding again. "*Che-che-che-che.*"

Julio felt for his bag. He had never been so weak. The effort of preparing the sling made him want to lie back down, but he must eat. He twirled the sling, and the stone wobbled through the air, bounced off a rock, and clattered downward. Chattering, the chipmunk ran away.

Julio lay back. He would try again, but later. Sun shining warm on his face, he looked out from his ledge, astonished to see that during his stupor it had snowed much more. Heavy, deep snow had completely covered his tracks.

Great mounds of snow hovered on drooping ponderosa branches. Only the feathery tracks of chipmunks and field mice had brushed the surface, and the telltale marks of a snowshoe rabbit.

Again it was spring. How long had he been sick? How many days behind the traders was he now? He was thirsty and hungry. His body ached as if he had been beaten, and he was so weak he could hardly stand. Wobbling like an old man, he gathered his things and backed over the shelf, the toes of Papá's boots scraping down the granite wall. At the base of the cliff his legs sank into snow halfway up his thighs, and he leaned against the stone, panting, eyes closed. But he had to push on. Had to find food. Had to find the wagons.

Something rustled in the bushes. Julio's eyes focused. His hand found the knife. Steadying himself, he waited, not moving.

From the shrubs came a sound, a whimper that was almost human. Whatever it was, it was hurt—an easy kill. Julio eased his load into the snow and inched closer to the sound. Breathing heavily, light-headed, he reached down and parted the branches, knife poised.

"Chivita!" The raspy whisper ripped through his throat. His knife slipped from his fingers. "Chivita! Chivita! Chivita!" Flinging snow aside, he burrowed into the bush and reached in to touch her. "Santa María, thank you! You heard my prayer!"

Chivita whined, weakly raising her head.

"Oh, Chivita, you're hurt! The Apaches—" Julio saw the gnawed shaft of an arrow protruding from her flank. "But they couldn't catch *you* either, could they, Little Goat?" With an arrow piercing her muscles, as sick—or sicker—than he had been, she had followed him all this way, finding his scent even through the snow and blizzard. Her tracks were covered. How long had she been here? How long had he tossed there on that ledge, out of his mind with fever? "Chivita, you'll be all right. You've got to be! I promise, Chivita, I will make you well."

He scooped the little animal from the bush, retrieved his knife, and carried her back up to his ledge. "Chivita, this will hurt," he whispered, stroking her head, "but I have to do it."

The wound was inflamed, oozing pus and blood. Chivita had tried to pull the arrow out with her teeth and had chewed through the shaft. There was barely enough wood left for Julio to grasp between his thumb and forefinger.

Chivita cried when he touched it.

"I'm sorry, Chivita." Taking his knife, he sliced deep into the putrid flesh and pried the arrow out. Chivita flinched but did not fight him.

"We must wash this and put medicine on it so you'll heal," he whispered, flinging the arrow over the ledge. "Then I'll bring water and food."

Caring for Chivita pushed Julio to do more than he

thought he could do. After he cleaned the wound and applied Mamá's medicine, he gathered wood, melted snow, killed a rabbit with his slingshot, gutted and skinned it, and boiled a rabbit stew in Papá's coffee pot. His fever returned, rose, fell. Sweat cooled his forehead.

As night approached, Julio felt his strength gradually coming back. The food had given him energy, Chivita's presence, new hope. The sun set, and soon stars filled the sky with chips of light so bright, he could see the dark shadows of trees against the gray-white snow.

Julio curled himself around Chivita and pulled the sarape over them. His fingers gently stroked past her ears, down her neck and front leg. As his thumb probed the smooth foot pads, Chivita's tongue scraped over his hand as if to say "Thank you."

"This warm breeze will eat up the snow, Chivita, soon. Tomorrow we'll find the trail and the wagons. We'll be all right. You'll see."

But he could not sleep. Now that he was not groggy from fever, the wound in his leg felt molten and throbbed under an unnatural pressure. He rolled toward the fire and pulled up the leg of his pants. The wolf had bitten, then torn. Scabs had formed over the tear, but a large flap of puffy, discolored skin was oozing pus around the partially sealed edge. It must have air to heal, Julio knew, and he could not risk infection. He had already used most of Mamá's medicine. Pinching the dead flesh, he pulled it up, uncovering the pus. With a flick of his knife, he sliced off the flap. Then he stabbed the tip of the blade into an ember and lifted it from the fire. Gritting his teeth against the pain, he shoved the ember, sizzling, onto the gush of fresh red blood.

Chapter Eight

Shafts of morning gray crept beneath Julio's eyelids, prying him awake. He lay unmoving, still and cold on his stone bed.

How close had he come to death? Apaches. Wolves. Blizzard. The wound, fever. No one would ever have known if he had died on this rock shelf. Mamá's prediction penetrated his memory: "You will die!"

Julio sat up. "Chivita! We've got to find those wagons!"

Chivita raised her head and whined weakly. Frenzied, Julio crawled about the ledge, thrusting his few possessions into his bag. Panic erased the pain in his leg, dispelling the lingering stupor. He jerked his sarape over his head, threaded the red sash through the handle of the coffee pot and the thongs of his sandals, and cinched it around his waist. His sombrero. Where was it? He'd tucked it in the sash yesterday—no, not yesterday—how many days ago? It must have dropped out along the way, buried now under three feet of fresh snow.

He knelt and smeared the last of Mamá's medicine first over Chivita's wound, then on his burn. "Chivita, come on, girl! Let's go!"

She raised her head, then lowered it again, shame unhidden in her brown eyes.

"It's all right, Chivita. You'll get stronger soon." She needed nourishment. They both did, but to hunt, to gather more firewood would take time, and they had already lost too many days. "We'll eat tonight," he promised, "when we reach the wagons." Hands shaking, Julio tugged Papá's sarape from beneath Chivita, folded it, and scooped Chivita inside. Grasping the rough sarape in both hands, he swung her over his shoulders like a lost lamb. Blood roared in his ears. He teetered, then leaned against the rock until the dizziness passed. It would be difficult, impossible, to balance in the deep snow without the use of his hands.

Chivita whimpered as Julio swung her down from his shoulders back onto the ledge. He worked his way off the cliff, Papá's boots sinking deep into the snow.

"Stay, Chivita. Stay." He lurched through the level layer of white to the trees. That and the effort of breaking green boughs from a pine left him trembling. He paused only long enough to catch his breath and scan the vacant valley. Then he stacked the boughs, thickest limbs forward, and wove them through with long switches of willow. It was like a travois, a primitive sleigh. He lifted Chivita down onto it and it slid smoothly over the snow, bearing her like a sarape-wrapped child.

With no trail to follow, no trace of wagons, only the occasional scurried tracks of field mice and the clover prints of ravens' feet, Julio headed north. Papá had said they would go north to the Arkansas River. He hoped he hadn't turned too soon. Each step pushed a heavy column of snow. Each breath tugged deeper into a tiredness that begged him to stop. Each thought, braided with his mother's warning, became a litany trudging through his mind: *Wagons, wagons, wagons or die, wagons or die, wagons or die, wagons—*

The sun, huge, bulbous, like the eye of an enormous buzzard, stared as if it were waiting to swoop down and devour him. Through the blur of his eyelashes the snow momentarily turned black, then bloodred. The sky, then the sun itself, faded to dark, then flashed back to light. The glare pricked at his eyes like jagged crystals of ice.

Sweat tracked across his neck. His feet and legs, strangled in Papá's boots, felt as if they were encased in great adobe blocks, immune to feeling. On and on he staggered through the blinding glare, pulling Chivita, sweating and cold. Unprotesting, Chivita rode behind. The muscles in Julio's shoulders and neck knotted and cramped. But the litany played: *Wagons or die...wagons...* He pushed on, his breath scraping against his throat. Later, he saw, in the distance, a large herd of elk, black against white, and deer—a doe and two spotted fawns—but too far away to tell.

Then he remembered nothing more until abruptly his foot hooked on something beneath the snow and he pitched forward. His face plunged deep into the cold, soothing darkness. Only the need to breathe made him stir. He turned his head, blew the snow from his nostrils, then closed his eyes, yielding to fatigue. The litany stopped.

Questions flitted through his mind and quickly disappeared, unanswered. How far had he walked in a daze without looking for the wagons?

He would think again. He would walk again. Later.

"Hunnn?"

Julio moaned. Sleep. Rest, only for a little while longer. So tired. So tired.

Chivita's breath ruffled his hair. Her wet tongue slopped across his face and hands.

He knew it was Chivita, but a bristling shadow leapt from his memory, confusing him. *Wolves!* Julio struck. His fist sank into bony flesh and fur, and Chivita yelped in pain.

"Oh, Chivi— I...sorry..." Julio squinted at her. His muscles drained into the snow, and he sank back, his head pounding.

Again Chivita's voice rumbled deep in her throat next to his ear.

Without uncovering his eyes Julio pushed her away. But she was insistent. Nudging beneath his arm, she shoved her wet nose against his lips.

Spluttering, Julio jerked his head to the side, pushed her again.

Chivita grabbed his shirt in her teeth and tugged, exposing skin to snow.

"Chivita!" His anger propelled him onto his elbow, but Chivita cowered just out of reach. "Fine for you!" Julio's voice cracked. "You didn't pull me all day." *Day!* Where was the sun?

Then, suddenly, he understood. "Chivita," he whispered, crawling to her, stroking her over and over, hugging her gently to his chest. "Chivita, I'm sorry. I'm sorry. "

In spite of the throbbing headache his mind slowly began to function again. If he had continued to sleep, he would not have awakened. Ever. He would have drifted away in the clear night without ever knowing. And there would have been no priest. Not for him, not for Papá. Ever.

Shivering, Julio pushed himself to his feet, surprised that the snow wasn't as deep as it had been that morning, surprised he hadn't noticed before. The last rays of sun were streaming up over the western horizon like purple vapor, coating the snow, sky, and trees. Julio blinked, but the blur remained.

The mountain slopes were sparsely covered with solitary ponderosa pines standing like sentinels against the fading light. "Wait, Chivita." Julio staggered through the snow to the nearest one. Still blinking to clear his vision, he paused to sniff the air. The strange purple glow from the sunset was dissolving, but the air seemed smoky, as if a haze covered everything. He squinted and sniffed, turned in a slow circle in the snow, but there was no dome of red glowing on the dark edge of the world, no scent of burning forest. Maybe it was his eyes.

He shrugged. He needed a fire. Dead wood snapped easily from the ponderosa, and the pile of kindling and branches grew quickly.

He squeezed his eyes shut, then opened them and blinked again. Nothing changed. His vision was still foggy, but he saw a jagged patch of auburn wood. It was a freshly gnawed porcupine chew halfway up a tree trunk. Porcupine, sluggish and slow, the easiest game to kill.

The porcupine had moved on, but it had left a path to the skeleton of another tree, which was cradling both dinner and the fuel for cooking it.

Darkness was coming on fast. The temperature was dropping. Coyotes had already begun their nightly chorus.

Julio pulled a heavy limb from the pile, sheared off the twigs, and tested its weight.

The porcupine on its hammock of dry limbs made no attempt to move away. Julio struck it hard across the nose, then, avoiding quills, raked it onto its back into the snow. Fingers trembling at the promise of food, he slit open its belly.

The flames of the fire were soon searing speared strips of meat. Faint from fatigue and from the tantalizing aroma, Julio sipped hot melted snow from Papá's coffee pot to keep himself from gobbling the meat half raw and scratched the itches that encircled his waist and crawled down his thawing legs.

When the meat was crisp and brown, juice sizzling into the fire, Julio held the first slice to cool. "Gracias." He gave thanks to the Lord, to the Virgin, to all the saints and angels.

When he and Chivita had eaten half the meat, Julio forced himself to stop, rationing what was left for breakfast. As soon as it was light, they would push on without hunting. Julio buried the meat under a layer of snow away from their bed and fire. He had plenty of wood to keep a hot flame burning all through the night.

Plenty of wood! He blinked, dodging the irritating smoke. *A whole tree of dead wood!* Why hadn't he thought of it sooner? If the wagons were anywhere near, they would see his fire, his huge fire. The bigger the fire, the farther it could be seen.

Strengthened by food, trembling with hope, Julio piled wood around the base of the dead tree and thrust a flaming torch inside. The fire crept slowly at first, then, crackling, it licked higher up the trunk into the dead branches until the whole tree glowed like a skeleton against the night.

Julio covered his smarting eyes. "See it!" he yelled to the men with the wagons. "See it. And come!"

Trying to control his giddiness, Julio slid the flute from his bag, licked his cracked lips, and circling, began to play. Chivita joined him in the familiar ritual, limping stiffly around the thick pile of fresh-smelling pine branches that would be their bed.

"So now you can walk again, eh, Little Goat?" Julio spoke softly. "That's good. Because tomorrow we will find those wagons. Or they will find us."

But beneath his words, like a drumbeat in his head, pulsed the litany *Wagons or die, wagons or die, wagons or die.*

Chapter Nine

It was deep night, the time when stillness is easily broken. Julio didn't know whether it was the piercing pain in his eyes or Chivita's bark that jolted him alert. He groped for the sling, forcing his eyes to open.

The glow of the two fires seeped beneath his lashes with a pain so terrible that he threw his arm over his eyes. The sling tumbled from his hand.

"Chivita!" he gasped. "I can't see!"

From the sound of it the animal on the other side of the fire was fairly large, maybe a bear. Its growl intertwined with Chivita's and grew louder. A stench of musk filled the air. It was the smell of a wolverine, fierce and ruthless, not an animal to tangle with.

Chivita barked again. Even without seeing her Julio

could tell she was jumping, darting, bounding from one side to the other, dodging the intruder's attacks.

"Chivita!" He forced his voice above the pain. "Chivita! Come here! Leave it alone!"

Chivita yelped, then Julio heard her dragging herself through the snow, small whimperings sounding in her throat. Panting, shaking, she huddled at his side.

Finding the sling where it had dropped in the pine boughs, Julio stood. Once again he tried to look, but the pain felt like sand scraping and tearing at his eyes. It was impossible to hold them open.

Heart pounding, he strained to hear. Whatever was out there was quiet now, watching. He could feel it looking at him. *It's out there, and I can't see! Don't know what it is! I can't see!*

"Shoot toward a sound; you don't need to see." It was Papá's voice, loud and clear in his head.

From across the crackling of the fire came a snarling, throaty *wuff* then the sound of rapid pawing. Julio's sling spun a rock. His scream rose with it, howling through his helplessness. It was a sound he could not stop. When it ended, Julio couldn't move. The animal would either attack or retreat.

The wolverine, snorting and huffing, dragged away the rest of the porcupine meat. It had gotten what it came for. Shaking, Julio breathed out and sank down beside Chivita. His head was splitting. The pain in his eyes was worse than a dozen wolf bites, worse than being seared by fire.

He groped in the direction of the sound of Chivita's licking. Words came out slowly. "You did it again, Little Goat, didn't you? Saved the flock." His fingers touched wet wiry hair. Blood, or only saliva? He touched his finger to his tongue. Blood. "You forgot you were hurt."

Exploring blindly over Chivita's body, he felt no dangerously deep slashes, but she flinched when he touched the place where he'd dug out the arrow. The wolverine's claws had gouged there again. "I'm sorry, Chivita." He stroked her head. It was difficult to think. Difficult now to do anything but give in to the pain. "There's no more medicine."

Crawling, he felt for wood to add to the fire, then he sat, cradling his aching head in his hand. *What's happening to me? Why can't I see?*

He thought back through the lost hours he'd plodded through the glaring sun reflecting on the snow. *Was it the snow? Did I look at it too long?* And finally the most terrifying question found words. *Will my eyes get better?*

"God," Julio whispered, "don't let me be blind. Chivita and I can't survive out here without my eyes." The fire flared up again, and Julio groaned. Even through closed eyelids the dancing flames stabbed and burned like a thousand tiny torches. He cupped snow against his eyes.

"How much more can we stand, Chivita?" He mumbled.

"Not much, I'm afraid. We're lost. Unless the wagons find us—" *Wagons or die*— "We'll never find them now. No food left, and I—I can't see to get wood. How can I defend us?"

Chivita nosed him and whined. "No, Little Goat. Not you either. You wouldn't survive another battle." He tied the red sash around Chivita's neck, then to his wrist, to be sure she didn't try to protect their camp again.

The night was endless, the pain in his eyes the most excruciating he had ever felt. Julio folded an edge of one sarape around his head to hold snow next to his eyes. But each time he began to drift into a tortured sleep, he awakened himself with moans. Chivita lay beside him with her chin propped on his arm, whimpering when he cried, licking his hands as if to give courage.

Julio awoke, his face pressed against prickly boughs. Saliva puddled under his lips. There were pine needles in his mouth. Little by little he became aware of the sensations of his body. Inside his head was a cross of cold, aching pain. Above the cross, like two flaming torches, his eyes.

He raised his eyebrows, trying to pull up his eyelids, but they wouldn't open. With the tips of his fingers he touched them. They were bulbous and swollen. The skin under his eyes was puffy. Pain, as severe as ever, intensified as the bright light of the morning sun shone through his closed eyelids.

Chivita was tugging impatiently against her unaccustomed leash. "No, Chivita!" Julio groaned. "I can't go. We have to stay here. Stay. And wait until..."

The tension on the sash relaxed. Chivita nudged him with her nose, then pawed at his hand. "What is it, Chivita?" he moaned.

Grimacing, he managed to peer through the narrow, watery slits of his eyes. What little he saw looked like wavy distortions under water. The image of sparkling snow swam into view. Then before him, not two paces away, colors, blurred colors, sorted themselves into parallel rows of red, white, and blue—tiny beads sewn onto the warm buff color of leather moccasins.

Chapter Ten

The man stood, not making a sound.

Fighting dizziness, light-headed from the pain in his eyes, Julio staggered to his feet. Facing the enemy, he brandished his knife, his eyes refusing to stay open in the glare from the sun.

The man laughed.

Confused, Julio stopped swinging but held the knife poised. From somewhere not far away came the sounds of horses, barking dogs, and the voices of women and children.

Then the man spoke. It was the deep, wheezy voice of an old man in a language Julio had never heard.

"No comprendo." Julio told him he couldn't understand. *What does he want? If he wanted to, he could have killed me in my sleep.* Julio shifted from one foot to the other, but the motion upset his balance, made him weave.

"No Spanish. English." The old voice wheezed. "You make signal?"

Startled by the switch in language, Julio struggled with the meaning of the heavily accented English words.

"Burn tree?"

The tree! Of course! He'd seen the burning tree.

"Yes." Cautiously Julio lowered the knife. "To get help."

"You American?"

"No." Julio shook his head, but the motion sent such pain through his eyes, that he grabbed his brow.

The old man put a hand on his shoulder, steadying him. The knife was plucked from Julio's grasp. Rough fingers were untying Chivita from his wrist, touching his face, around his eyes. The gruff voice seemed to fade away, come and go, spiral closer, push forward a few words— "...eyes..." "...snow..." —then disappear into the distance. Something cold and dark was wrapped around his head. The darkness spread from his eyes, over his ears, into his thoughts, and he felt himself sinking.

When he awoke, a woman was leaning over him. He could hear her humming the way Mamá hummed when she spun. The heat from the woman's body, like the weight of his headache, pressed down on him. He reached up to take the blindfold from his eyes.

Clucking, the woman swatted his hand away, then unleashed a string of words he couldn't understand. Gently she removed the blindfold and immediately replaced it with another that smelled strongly of herbs.

"Gracias." Julio tried to sit up. "Muchas gracias. Thank you." His slanted bed intensified the throbbing pressure on his feet. "¿Quién es usted? Who are you? Where's my dog? How long have I been here?"

Laughing and scolding, the woman pushed him back down, not answering in either language. The bed jostled. From above his head came the swish of a tail and a distinctive horsey smell.

"My feet..." he complained, trying once more to sit up. The woman's hand was firm on his chest, holding him down. The tail swished again, and the air filled with the warm smell of fresh manure plopping into snow.

Julio pointed blindly toward his feet and made a sound that in any language would be understood—a long, pitiful moan.

The woman pushed off his chest with a shove, circled to his feet, and began to twist and tug on Papá's boots. Julio clenched his teeth and was about to cry out when she stopped. A blade touched his bare ankle, and before he could object, she had sliced the leather, and one foot, then the other, was free.

"Ahch!" she exclaimed. He heard Papá's boots land somewhere in the snow. Julio could imagine what she had found. Frostbite, maybe. Certainly chilblains—swollen, split skin on the sides of his toes that itched and burned— and raw blisters. And a smell probably worse than the one near his head. The woman washed and dabbed at his feet, up his ankles, scolding more and more loudly until she was silenced by the scabbed-over wolf bite.

Julio sighed and wiggled his freed toes in the fresh air and sunshine. Chattering close to his face, the woman adjusted the eye covering. She poked his chest with a blunt finger, slapped the horse's rump, and then she was gone. The horse—and Julio's bed—shifted. He and the horse were connected. He was on a travois made from the same lodge poles and buffalo skin that were raised as tipis at night. Now it carried him like one more shaggy buffalo hide.

From nearby came the whispers of children. Julio felt them watching him. Caught in the euphoria of well-being, he waved and called out, "¡Hola! Hello! How are you? I have lots of sisters your age. Eight of them. Eight!"

The whispers exploded into giggles that bounded away. Then, so quiet he could scarcely feel whether it was the brush of a tiny breeze or the motion of a person, he sensed someone near. "Hello? Hello!" The load beside him on the travois shifted slightly. "Chivita?" There was no answer, only the hush of retreating moccasins against powdery dust.

Who are these people? What will they do with me? For

a few moments the woman had made him feel safe. But from the way she moved and mumbled under her breath, she seemed old. How safe could he be under the protection of an old Cheyenne woman? *Safe like the lamb is safe with the wolf.* He remembered the last time he let himself feel comfortable. If it hadn't been for Chivita, he would have frozen to death. His hand reached toward his eyes.

The horse at his head snorted. The old woman's voice came back into range, talking to herself, or him, or the horse. Grumbling, she mounted. Other horses whinnied and stomped. Dogs barked. The travois lurched, jerking him forward, headfirst. Behind the horse's sloshy steps the travois slid over snow and scraped against the patches of exposed earth beneath. He wondered how long he had been riding on this twisting carriage.

These people didn't have to help me, Julio realized, again feeling gratitude toward the woman and the old man with the wheezy voice. *They could have left me, killed me. Without my sight Chivita and I wouldn't have lived much longer.* But, he reminded himself again, *they are savages like the Arapaho and Apache, not to be trusted. The lambs. El Río de las Animas Perdidas en Purgatorio. Papá. I should have a weapon, be prepared.* His hands slid down his sides and across the pile of hides beneath him. They were large pelts, probably buffalo, and smelled of wood smoke and dust. His fingertips bumped the hard surface of an earthenware jar, then traced the roughly woven strips of a rawhide basket. Closer to him he felt the short-haired pelt of a beaver, then soft leather and a strap. It was his own leather bag. His sarape was beneath it. He felt again. All his things were there, everything except his sandals. Had they been tossed out along the trail with Papá's boots? Even his knife was back in the sheath at his waist. So he wasn't a prisoner, not if they allowed him his knife. *But they're not to be trusted.*

Julio heard the laughter of children and the barking of dogs drawing closer. One after another, the children dashed by, touching, poking, slapping him.

The old woman yelled at them. The horse lurched ahead, breaking its pace, and the child warriors dashed away. Strange. Julio listened more intently. He'd heard only the voices of women and children and a few old men. Where were the young men?

Chivita jumped on the travois beside him, panting. Her nose prodded his neck and ear, whiskers tickling.

"What a deserter you are, Chivita! Have you been making new friends? At least you've healed enough to walk on your own." His fingers slid down her side to the reinjured wound as she snuggled against him. "At least," he said, "you can see. You may have to learn to be my eyes, too, Little Goat. Maybe forever."

He slid the woman's bandage onto his forehead. Even with the lids squeezed closed, the brightness stung through like coarse salt. Breathing deeply, he forced his eyelids to open. Brightness and blur. Snow and no snow. Dark and light. Something brown up close, too fuzzy to identify. Stifling a groan, he pulled the bandage back into place. His vision was no better. The pain was the same.

He fingered Teresita's white stone, and his mind wandered back home, to a time long ago. He was only six or seven. It was a Sunday. The mass had been a special celebration. Father Martínez was wearing heavy green robes and sashes embroidered with gold thread and had a great pointed hat on his head. Julio edged his way along the cool wall toward the chancel.

"Pardon me, Father."

He remembered how Father Martínez had looked around.

"Here I am."

When Father Martínez spotted Julio, he threw back his head and laughed, dislodging the hat and startling the sparrows in the vigas overhead.

Julio showed him the tiny coin, balanced on the tip of his finger, and asked him what it said. The priest held the coin near a bank of flickering candles and squinted at the imprint of the lady in long skirts, holding a flag. Then he turned it over to the side with the letters and numbers. "Why, it's American!" He sounded surprised. "A silver half dime." He said "half dime" in English, then, frowning, he looked Julio straight in the eyes and said in English, "Where did this come from?"

"No sé—I don't know." Julio still remembered how strange it was for the priest to talk to him in that other language. "Papá me la dio. Papá gave it to me."

"You're Enrique Montoya's boy, no?"

"Sí."

From that time on Father Martínez had always spoken to him in English.

But now Teresita had his coin, and Papá's grave smothered the question neither Papá nor the priest had answered. *You want to know what's out here, Teresita?* he thought, rubbing his hands across his itching skin. *It's just what Mamá said. Wilderness. Wolves. Death. Even when I get to Bent's Fort*—

Then with a jolt the daydream was over. He had not been thinking clearly at all. True, the tribe seemed to be traveling downslope. True, they seemed to be headed northeastward. But he had no idea where they were going.

Chapter Eleven

It was the first time Julio had been inside a tipi. Even though he was unable to see it, the round wall felt as if it were pressing in, suffocating him with the scent of stale smoke. The old woman had left him here with his possessions, including the tattered sandals.

Chivita's leg thumped on the dirt floor as she dug at her neck.

"You itch, girl?" he asked, scratching behind her ear. "Me too."

He could feel Chivita's leg continue to flail, then freeze in midair.

"What is it, Little Goat?"

Itch forgotten, Chivita sprang to her feet and growled. Julio heard, too, and felt the vibration through the ground.

Hooves, pounding. Did buffalo stampede at night? Or herds of antelope? Were they horses? An attack?

Julio jerked the bandage from his eyes and drew his knife. Outside, people began to yell.

A shot rang out, then another. Wild screams ripped through the approaching thunder.

"Santa María!" Julio cried, flattening himself on the floor, arm pressed over Chivita. Images — Apaches, Papá, the stream — flashed inside his eyelids. It was impossible to force his eyes to stay open.

The horses circled so closely their hooves peppered the outside of the tipi with clods of dirt. Around and around they thundered, their riders whooping and shooting. Then as suddenly as they had approached, they stopped. A drum began to throb and a single voice sang out.

Julio breathed more deeply. His pulse slowed to a normal pace. He lifted the skirt of the tipi and tried to peer out, but he could see only a blur of dark silhouettes against the campfire. A woman shrieked over the unwavering drumbeat. Like moths, the blurs began to circle the flame, dancing, dancing on and on. Deep into the night the dance, the woman's keening, the incessant beat of the drum.

After a sleepless night Julio found the morning stretched out long and quiet. His stomach had been growling for a long time when the old woman pushed him down on a log and put something in his hand. Food. Breakfast or maybe lunch. It was a small cake made of dried berries, some combination of serviceberries and chokecherries, he thought, and plums, held together with fat. He was still eating when he heard the old woman's voice and the voices of men talking loudly. It sounded like the beginning of a fight.

The talk moved toward him. From along the riverbank children came laughing and running. Julio's shoulders tightened. The berry cake in his mouth went dry. He had accepted his place with the tribe as additional luggage belonging to the old woman. Except for her and the children—and the silent one he'd heard alongside the travois—he'd gotten used to being ignored. But last night the men had returned, and now he was to be dealt with. He dropped the sticky cake and stood up, slowly.

More people pressed in around him, talking. The old woman, then others kept repeating a word that sounded like *Véʔhoʔe* and seemed to have something to do with him. Twice he heard the wheezy voice of the old man who had found him. "Véʔhoʔe! Véʔhoʔe!" he insisted, poking Julio with a stiff finger, then tugging a shock of his hair. Then it was the old woman again, thumping Julio's chest.

Julio had never imagined knowing people by their touch, but this was undoubtedly the old woman touching him. She caressed his cheek and jaw with her rough fingers and twitched the hair at the back of his neck. Her hand slid across his shoulder, then down his arm, gripping and squeezing while she talked. Unsettling thoughts pushed up from his memory—stories of women claiming prisoners to replace lost mates and sons.

"Speak English?" A new, male voice, deep and powerful, cut through the old woman's chatter.

This must be the chief, Julio thought. "A little."

"American?"

"No." Julio's fingers twitched toward the knife. He forced them to be still.

"Texan?"

"No."

"*Français?*"

"No, I'm Mexican, from Taos."

Several voices exploded in a fast—paced discussion, and he heard that word Vé?ho?e again. Fingers explored his sarape and sash, touched his hair. He fought the urge to jerk away.

"Not Mexican!" He wished he could see the owner of this powerful voice.

"Yes, I'm Mexican," he repeated. "Julio Montoya, from Taos. What tribe are you?"

"Tse-tsėhésė! Cheyenne." He drew one of Julio's index fingers across the other three times.

People shifted positions, and Julio heard someone move forward through the crowd.

"¿Verdad? Usted es mejicano?" It was the smooth,

serious-sounding tone of a young man, asking in Spanish, "Is it true? You're Mexican?"

Julio felt the muscles in his shoulders relax. After all this time here was someone who spoke his own language. "Yes! I left Taos..." Briefly he told where he had come from, where he was going.

"Bent's Fort? Alone? From Taos it's very far."

"No, I didn't leave alone."

"Did the sun on snow burn your eyes?" the young voice asked.

As if it had a will of its own, Julio's hand lifted to the bandage. "Yes—" He hesitated, his need to know battling with his fear of knowing. The weight tilted. "My eyes... Will they heal?"

The voice repeated Julio's question in Cheyenne. The man Julio thought was the chief spoke, then the old woman, then the chief talked again for a long time. The back of Julio's neck prickled. The berry cake twisted in his stomach.

"Néške?e will heal your eyes. And your leg and feet." The young voice ended the tension. "It is decided. Julio, you will travel with us, the Tse-tsėhésė.

We are going to trade buffalo hides with the husband of Owl Woman, William Bent."

"William Bent!" Julio exclaimed. "Where?"

"Bent's Fort on the Arkansas River."

"Ah!" The sound exploded from Julio's throat. *These*

*are the Cheyenne Papá talked about! And they're going
to Bent's Fort! A woman from this tribe is William Bent's
wife. I will see again! My eyes will heal. I will find a
priest.*

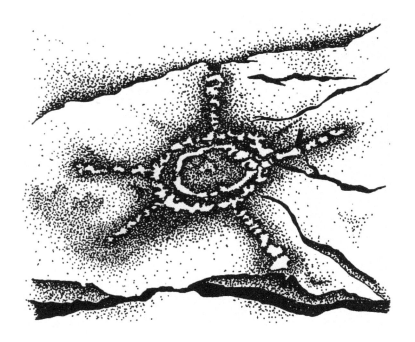

Chapter Twelve

The next two days were the strangest days of Julio's life. He was dragged along behind a plodding horse, sightless, blindfolded, pampered by an old woman he'd never seen and who never stopped talking. He resigned himself, for now, to wait for his eyes to heal. Sometimes he played his flute. The children still came around to touch, then run—and once or twice Julio was sure he heard other soft steps whispering alongside.

From time to time the young man walked beside him, sometimes in silence, sometimes talking with him in Spanish, always serious. His name was Dancing Feather.

Dancing Feather described the buffalo tracks that marked the plains. He explained how the warriors had returned that night from a battle with the Kiowa. "The

woman was screaming because her son died in the battle."
Then his voice became intense, forceful."He died in the
manner of the ancient Tse-tsėhėsė. He died a good death,
with honor." At the naming of his tribe Dancing Feather's
tone carried the same fierce pride as the chief, White
Buffalo, his father.

Dancing Feather told Julio when they came to a wide
slash of wagon ruts that marked a trail. He taught him
to say, in Cheyenne, "E-peva?e—thank you. It is good."
And he asked about his family in Taos.

"Yes. I miss them, especially my sister Teresita. We are
the same age."

"Twins?"

"No." Julio did not mention his father.

On the evening of the second day the old woman was
fussing and scolding over the healing scabs on Julio's legs
and feet, washing, drying, patting, shooing Chivita away.
He thought she was finished, but she was not. Something
felt like warm, melted butter and slid first over one foot,
then over the other. As the woman tugged, Julio realized
what he felt was the smooth caress of leather moccasins
exactly the size of his feet. He reached down. His fingers
traced the tiny stitches and the rows of beads. "E-peva?e!
E-peva?e! So that's where my sandals were!" he said.
"You used them to measure for these. They feel wonderful!
Thank you." He knew she couldn't understand a word he
said.

Prattling, the old woman moved his head. When she unwrapped the last bandage from Julio's eyes, he said the words again. "E-peva?e. E-peva?e." He wanted to say more.

It was early evening. The pain in his eyes was almost gone. Even though it was near dark, he was dazzled by the light. The grinning figure before him swam into a blurry focus. Her teeth were polished, and her smile glittered like the smile of a young girl, but her old, weathered skin was crisscrossed with scars. He wondered what had happened to her.

"Mo?öhtavė-hohpe?" She lifted Papá's coffee pot from the travois and waved it in front of his blurry eyes. "Mo?öhhtavė-hohpe?" she asked again, her wrinkles pushing into a smile. Julio blinked, still trying to focus.

He swung his legs over the edge of the travois and stood unsteadily in the soft moccasins, seeing his traveling companions for the first time. "Dancing Feather?" he asked the old woman. His hand reached to his waistband, scratching an itch.

Chattering and flailing her arms, the woman scuttled away. Julio looked about him. The caravan was almost as he'd envisioned—horses pulling travois, men and some women on horseback, some gathering wood. Lodgepoles were already being raised for the night. But the plains! They were nothing like he'd imagined.

He stared in disbelief at the flat, treeless prairie

surrounding him on three sides. It stretched so far, the sky seemed to wrap under the land's end. He had never seen so far before. In the west the mountains he had come from towered huge and blue against an orange and pink and purple sunset.

His eyes drank in the colors, the shapes. "Gracias," he murmured aloud, his face upturned. "Thank you, Santa María." More now than when he couldn't see, he realized what a loss his vision would have been.

"Can you see?"

Julio turned to the tall young man with a broad chest and strong arms who was walking toward him.

"Dancing Feather?" Julio blinked to clear his vision, but this time his eyes were not tricking him. Neither were the rays of the sunset. Dancing Feather's long black hair was streaked with gray, but he was young, Julio guessed, about his own age. His body was thick, muscular. Three parallel white scars arched above his right elbow, and from a leather thong around his neck hung the largest single bear claw Julio had ever seen.

"Good. Now you can see again." Dancing Feather nodded his head toward the old woman. She was clutching Papá's coffee pot in her hand. "Néške?e likes coffee," he explained.

"Néške?e," he repeated, smiling.

"All Tse-tséhése like this black soup," Dancing Feather said. "Néške?e wants to know, do you have coffee beans?"

"Mo?òhtavè-hohpe?" Néške?e asked again.

Julio shook his head. "I'm sorry," he said. He tried to answer in Cheyenne. "No Mok Pi."

Néške?e howled with laughter at his mistake.

"Mo?—òh—tavè—hohpe," she repeated slowly, emphasizing each syllable with a thump on his chest. "Mo?—òh—tavè—hohpe."

Julio repeated it, this time correctly, and Néške?e grinned and said something to Dancing Feather.

"Dancing Feather—" Julio wiggled his foot from side to side. "Please tell her I thank her for making these moccasins."

Dancing Feather translated, then, as Néške?e was still talking, said, "Néške?e says she did not make them."

"Then, who did?" Again, Julio's hand dived to his waist after the itch. Néške?e broke off in mid-sentence. Her smile vanished. "Ohohyaa!"

Before Julio could think of backing away, Néške?e had grabbed the waist of his pants and pulled down. "Ohohyaa!" she growled, pointing, jabbering to Dancing Feather.

Julio struggled to cover himself, tried to escape, but her grip on him was as unyielding as a beaver trap.

Dancing Feather turned away. "Go with Néške?e," he said.

Sounds of laughter followed them as she marched him at arm's length into the cottonwoods along the river.

Chivita barked and danced around them as if it were a game.

"Néške?e," Julio protested, unable to wrench his arm free. "You've been good to me. Thank you. E-peva?e. ¡Gracias! Merci." He tried all the thank-yous he knew. "But I'm not your prisoner! I'm too young to marry you! You're too old! I want to become a priest! Please, let go of me!" If she'd been a man, he might have escaped, but he was afraid of hurting her. "Néške?e! What are you doing?"

In the cover of the cottonwoods Néške?e tugged at his clothes. He was clutching them to him, struggling to get away when she released his arm. Her fists dug into her hips and she stepped back, haranguing him with words he could not understand. She reached out, turned up the torn bottom edge of his shirt, and pointed at the inside seam.

Julio gaped. All along the seam tiny rows of pearls shone in the twilight. "Ugh!" he exclaimed, checking his waistband. He strained to focus on the nearly transparent lice squirming against his skin. He was crawling with them, and well supplied with eggs for the generations to come. All Néške?e wanted was to wash his clothes.

Meekly he followed her instructions. He slipped off the moccasins, then backed into the chilly river, tossed her the two sarapes, his shirt, the sash from his waist, and his pants. He stood there in the water, shivering, embarrassed, naked as a baby, while she scrubbed his clothes with the roots of a yucca plant. When she threw a root to him and pointed to his hair, he washed with it, too, not only his hair but his whole body, sudsing and rinsing over and over to get rid of the vermin.

"Come here, Chivita!" he called. "Your turn." Chivita splashed into the water, and Néške'e laughed as Julio took the yucca root to Chivita's bristly coat. "Once you get used to it, Little Goat," he mumbled, "it feels pretty good."

Néške'e washing clothes in the river made Julio think of home. Mamá, his sisters, and other women and girls, laughing, gossiping, quarreling among themselves as they pounded and scrubbed clothes on river rocks. What would they be doing now? Would they be thinking about him? "I miss you," he whispered. "And you still don't know about Papá."

Chapter Thirteen

Wet but clean clothes clinging, Julio walked back toward the camp. Little boys were rolling large hoops made with green willow branches. Others were shooting play arrows at the centers of the moving hoops. When they saw Julio and Chivita, they laughed and followed, pretending to scratch all over their bodies. They didn't follow for long.

Several girls who were older than the boys came running toward them carrying baskets and shouting. The girl in front was pointing, her long hair shimmering behind her like a raven's wings in the purple hue of sunset. When she saw Julio, her deep-brown eyes widened. Her pace faltered, and she stopped. The other girls gestured and the boys dropped their games, turned, and everyone ran on toward the river leaving Julio alone with the girl. Her glance flickered down to his feet. A big smile spread across her face and wrinkled the top of her nose.

Julio looked down too. "You!" He glanced up from his moccasins into her twinkling eyes. "You made these for me! Thank you! E-peva'e."

The girl's smile stretched even wider, and her hair bounced as she ran on.

Julio retraced his steps to the river to see what was happening. Quietly now the boys were following one another along the bank to the left, the girls to the right. Slipping out of their moccasins, they waded into the water, boys facing the older girls. At a signal from the girl with the raven hair, the boys began to shout and beat the surface of the water with their hands, moving forward. Deftly the girls scooped up basketfuls of fleeing fish.

He needed time to think. "Come on, Chivita," Julio said, patting the wet pants on his legs. Chivita shook herself and followed Julio into the privacy of the woods, the voices of the boys still ringing out behind them.

In some ways he had felt better when he was suspicious of these Cheyenne, when he thought they like the Apache, were his enemies. "But I was wrong, Chivita. Néške'e just wanted to help us. Why did that girl make me moccasins? I don't even know her name. Nobody has asked anything of us at all—except coffee."

Néške'e, Dancing Feather, the girl, the ones Mamá and

the church called "pagan," dressed in different clothes, could have been his neighbors in Taos. It was confusing. He was Mexican and Catholic. The life of the Cheyenne should not seem so—acceptable, especially...His fists tightened. He made himself remember what happened to Papá.

Thump! A small object bounced off his shoulder. Julio glanced up into the trees. *Thump!* This time off his arm. He turned. In the clearing stood the girl, dripping wet, poised to throw another pebble.

"Hey! Why are you doing that?" But she didn't answer. Grinning, she gestured with her head, "Come on."

Returning to the campsite, he saw men sitting on the smooth white trunks of fallen cottonwood trees, resting and talking as the women worked. Some of the dogs had been put to work, too, carrying loads of branches for the fire. Julio started to gather wood, but the women giggled and jabbered at him, and Dancing Feather called, "Julio, come over here! That's the women's work. Come, sit with us."

Julio eased into the circle of men but couldn't understand their conversation. For a while Dancing Feather translated the talk about buffalo, but then he seemed to forget. Julio noticed again the raised scars on Dancing Feather's arm and wondered about the bear claw around his neck. Several of the old men were leaning over a game of bone dice. Near where the women were preparing fish, little girls played with beaded dolls with human hair. The dolls looked like copies of themselves. Little girls playing with dolls—they reminded Julio of Rosita and Alicia and Gabriela Ultima. After so much darkness Julio feasted his eyes on everything he could see.

Cheyenne women were different from his mother and sisters. Their straight suede dresses covered them from their necks to their ankles, the right sides of the skirts hanging longer than the left. The dresses were fringed, he supposed, like the leather clothing of trappers, to funnel rainwater off the leather.

Smiling broadly, Néške?e came toward him offering a crisp trout speared on a willow branch.

"E-peva?e, Néške?e." Julio stood up, but the men grumbled.

"Sit down!" Dancing Feather said. "Too much *e-peva?e.*"

Julio took the willow spear and eased down, glancing sideways. Néške?e brought another fish, then another and another, and he, like everyone else, ate until he could eat no more.

The fire dried his clothes, and as the moon rose, Julio saw it was almost full. The last time he'd seen it, on the night of the burning tree, it had been only a fuzzy blur. Warm, and as comfortable as he could be in company he couldn't understand, Julio slid to the ground and leaned back against the log.

The women were busy building up the fire, cleaning
the campsite. Julio's thoughts drifted home as he began to
watch them again. How different they were. Their clothes
were modest, not like the low-cut blouses and frilly veils
of the women of Taos. The Cheyenne women's faces were
the color nature had made them, not disguised with alegría
juice or powdered deer antler. They didn't smoke corn
shuck cigarillos. Julio let his eyes follow the slender girl
with long black hair, who was carrying a load of wood.

Julio was startled by Dancing Feather's nudge.
"What?"

"The men want to know what you're looking at,"
Dancing Feather said.

"Nothing!" Julio felt heat rise to his face. "I was just
watching. I couldn't understand what you were saying."

"Then you should learn Cheyenne."

"All right." Julio scooted back up the log. "How do you
say, 'How do you say…?'?"

"Na-me?-tonėšenėheve…?" Dancing Feather said. "
Na-me?-tonėšenėheve…"

Julio pointed to first one thing and then another, asking
the men, " Na-me?-tonėšenėheve…?" Obviously enjoying
the entertainment, they answered Julio's question again
and again and again until the old man who had found Julio
in the snow leaned forward. He pointed a gnarled finger at
the girl Julio had been watching.

"Na-me?-tonesenėheve…?" he wheezed, switching the

rules. Julio shook his head.

"Tell him, 'Emoonae,'" Dancing Feather whispered in his ear.

"Emoonae," Julio repeated, and the men all burst into laughter. They slapped their legs and slapped one another and pointed.

"It means 'beautiful,'" Dancing Feather said. Everyone was laughing now, the women, the children, everyone except Julio. And the girl. Fingers were pointing at him, and he could hear the word *emoonae* repeated as the story was retold by one to another around the circle.

"It is true, Dancing Feather." Julio's voice rose over the jumble of sound. "Tell them the girl *is* emoonae. Her spirit is emoonae. She made these for a blind stranger with injured feet." He slid his moccasined feet through the dust toward the fire. "What is her name? She has never told me."

"Silent Walker."

"E-peva?e, Silent Walker," Julio said, nodding.

"Ha ho!" Again the men laughed, but now fingers pointed toward Dancing Feather. Dancing Feather's shoulders squared. He held his head stiffly erect as the bear claw swung to a stop on his chest.

Julio reached into his leather bag. Gift giving, he knew, was a custom among the Plains people. He'd heard the traders and trappers talking about how important it was to give and receive. He had received.

What could he give in return? His fingers touched Teresita's lucky stone. He couldn't give that away. What else did he have except that and his ragged clothing? Touching the coffee pot stirred memories: the morning he'd first seen Romeo's pack, the first campfire he and Papá had made, the first hot coffee they'd brewed, Papá's grave, the rabbit stew he'd made for Chivita...Even dented and black, his gift would be Papá's coffee pot. It was the gift of his journey.

"Please, Dancing Feather, give this to Silent Walker from me. I'm sorry it is not new like my moccasins, but it is all I have."

As Silent Walker understood, her face lit up. Her eyes sparkled. She smiled and made a sign—probably thank-you—with her hand, and then the other women crowded around her gift, touching it and exclaiming.

"Julio." Julio's head jerked up. Everyone was looking at him as Dancing Feather spoke, but no one was laughing now. "My father, White Buffalo, says for one so young you are wise. He says you are brave like the Tse-tséhésé." Dancing Feather's hand touched the bear claw. "You battled wolves, the snow, and the sun. Tomorrow, he says, you will go with the men."

One by one the men stood, chatting now among themselves, and moved away from the light of the fire toward the tipis. Without another word or gesture to Julio, Dancing Feather left too. Néške?e was nowhere to be seen. What did the Tse-tsėhésė expect of him now that he could see?

Bewildered, Julio gathered up his leather bag and the sarapes Néškeʔe had spread near the fire to dry.

"Come, Chivita," he said softly, reaching into the bag for his flute. He tiptoed into the trees to find a place to spend the night, once again, alone.

Chapter Fourteen

The next day, before they left camp, Dancing Feather had said again, "Julio, you are brave like the Tse-tséhésé. You're not afraid to die. Come." They traveled east on foot, men only.

It wasn't until they reached a wooded strip beside a stream that Dancing Feather told him about the Cheyenne ceremony that night. "Spirits will come—from the north, the south, the east, and the west," he said. "We will be purified and see visions."

Julio knew he should not stay for this pagan ritual. He should have gone as soon as he'd realized what was going to happen. But White Buffalo had said something to Dancing Feather in Cheyenne, and Dancing Feather had gone away.

White Buffalo was picking and discarding stones from beside the stream and mounding them in a pile. His face was daubed with red, the wrinkles the only sign of his age.

White Buffalo looked up at Julio and pointed, first to the fallen trees and branches by the stream, then to the ground by the fire circle, signaling him to gather firewood with the other young men.

"I—I'm sorry, White Buffalo," Julio stammered. "I—I'm Catholic. I can't do this—this ceremony with you. My religion is different. I have to become a Catholic priest so Papá—" The words tumbled out unbidden. "Papá was killed on the trail, and I—"

White Buffalo placed his hands on Julio's upper arms. "Is this why you were traveling alone?" His voice rumbled deep and warm. "Julio, here you will learn to see with the eyes of your heart. The spirit of your father is free."

Julio started. It was the first time White Buffalo had called him by name, the first time he had spoken to him since his eyes had healed. "The stones," White Buffalo said, pointing to the pile he had accumulated, "they are old, old spirits. Good medicine. They will not harm you."

Julio backed away as White Buffalo raised a skull-shaped stone, turning it over and over in his hands to examine every pore.

I'll leave. I'll go on to Bent's Fort alone, Julio thought, glancing up at White Buffalo, but White Buffalo's eyes were riveted on his, holding him as he raised a slender finger and pointed once again. Stream. Fire circle. Julio went to work.

The supply of wood grew. Back and forth, back and forth Julio went, quieting his thoughts with the rhythm. When the stack of wood beside the fire circle was as tall as he was and the length of a horse, White Buffalo motioned for him and the other wood gatherers to stop. Julio sat down on a stump, willing Dancing Feather back. Something strange had happened between him and White Buffalo. Now he could not simply walk away.

On his right, two rows of rocks outlined a pathway from the fire circle to a pit dug neatly into the ground. In front of the pit, dirt was piled into a mound, and on top lay the bleached skull of a buffalo with the dark horn coverings still intact. Nearby stood the bare frame of the lodge, the curved boughs laced into a dome.

White Buffalo began to place the wood over the mound of stones, the tip of each piece pointing to the sky. He treated the wood with the same reverence as he had the stones, as if he were speaking with a spirit inside. He stuffed handfuls of dry grass among the bleached limbs, and the fire was ready to light.

Julio felt his body stiffen as several men lifted the small lodge into position over the pit. The ceremony was about to begin. *Come on! Dancing Feather, come on!*

White Buffalo gave an order. The men lifted hides over the bent-willow dome, overlapping the edges, then weighted them to the ground with rocks.

In the west the sun inched closer to the distant snow-covered mountains. It slipped from behind clouds to paint the faces of those who stood in silence, arms folded across their chests. Others carried water from the stream to dampen the ground around the fire circle.

A shiver raced down Julio's spine when White Buffalo's sudden chant echoed out into the twilight. Flame blazed from his hand to the dry grass and wood. The fire roared. Within the fire circle the stones began to heat. Again and again White Buffalo piled on more wood until the stones became so hot they glowed red. As the fire burned down, the first stone was scraped from the coals and rolled down the rock-lined path. The stone bearer knelt at the opening of the lodge and pushed it into the pit inside.

White Buffalo entered alone and closed the flap. Soon Julio heard what he thought must have been a kind of prayer chanted within. It reminded him of Father Martínez chanting the liturgy in the Taos church. After moments of silence the low flap opened, White Buffalo crawled out, and a second stone was added to the pit. After the third stone White Buffalo again entered and prayed.

The men gathered. Two eagles circled high above the hills to the south—a good sign for the Cheyenne, Papá had said, but it had not been a good sign for Papá and him. Julio wiped his sweaty palms against his pants.

White Buffalo spoke to the assembled group and pointed toward a profusion of silvery sage bushes growing on the plain. White Buffalo bowed and crossed his arms over his chest, and the men moved away one by one, into the bushes.

"Julio!" As if from nowhere Dancing Feather was beside him.

"Where have you been? I can't do this!" Dancing Feather motioned for him to be quiet and to follow him into the sage. "But Dancing Feather..." Dancing Feather's hand chopped through the air, commanding silence.

Julio followed. The smell of sage surrounded him as he brushed past the spindly silver-green leaves, and he watched as Dancing Feather moved from plant to plant, finally selecting one. Standing before the sage, Dancing Feather said, "Ha ho," and spoke words Julio didn't know, then broke off several twigs, held them in front of his face, and inhaled deeply.

He turned toward Julio. "To breathe through," he whispered, again lifting the sage to his face. "You gather some too."

"Dancing Feather, you don't understand. I can't. I'm Catholic, I..."

Dancing Feather's eyes grew darker. He pointed again to the sage.

Ay! God, help me! Julio prayed silently. He could not leave now. With God's help he would endure. But if Father Martínez and the Church ever found out, they might not let him become a priest. He moved through the sage, stopped, and reluctantly reached out.

"No." Dancing Feather touched his arm. "First ask, then say, 'Ha ho.' " He gestured toward the bush and repeated the words he had said before.

Does he mean for me to ask the sage if I can pick it? Thank it, as if it had a spirit?

Julio stared at the silvery leaves on their brittle stems. It was as if he had never seen sage before.

Maybe this life does have a spirit. It is the feeling I have for my sheep and the nighthawk, and for Chivita— especially for Chivita. And what does she know of religion? Nothing. Even less than Dancing Feather and his people. Maybe knowing or not knowing doesn't make any difference at all. Or maybe—again his anger at Saint Christopher flamed inside his chest—maybe religion confuses what Chivita and the sage already know. They aren't afraid to die without a priest's final rites.

Filled with a strange confusion, Julio looked into the dark eyes of his companion. He reached toward the bush. "Gracias," he said aloud. "Ha ho." He snapped off seven pieces of sage and, holding them like a bouquet to his nose, inhaled the sharp fragrance.

"Let's go," Dancing Feather said quietly and turned

again toward the open meadow. In the dusk the embers of the fire glowed, luring Julio toward the unknown.

All the men had returned now, each clutching sage. Julio counted. Including Dancing Feather and himself, they were twelve.

The evening sky darkened into night. Silence descended upon the gathering. White Buffalo raised his arms to the sky and, in a harsh, solemn voice, began.

Chapter Fifteen

All the men but two removed their clothing and hung loincloths, blankets, and moccasins on the willows and fallen cottonwoods by the stream. One of the men who had not undressed carried a large gourd into the lodge.

Julio slipped his sarape over his head, removed his shirt, moccasins and, last, his pants, and rolled them into a bundle, which he clutched in front of him. His skin gleamed white in the light of the fire like the underbelly of a fish.

Dancing Feather leaned toward Julio, speaking softly. "Julio, when we go in the lodge we say—" And he said a long, difficult word—or phrase—Julio couldn't tell which. "It means many things: Great Spirit. Earth Mother. Everything above and everything below…We say this when we go in or out of the lodge. Or if we need to leave during the ceremony." Dancing Feather knelt, the bear claw dangling from his neck, and saying the sacred word, crawled inside. Julio drew a deep breath, set his bundle of clothes on a branch, and followed him into the mouth of the lodge, into heat and blackness.

Around the pit of rocks there was scarcely room to sit cross-legged without burning his feet or knees. He drew up into himself, muscles taut, trying not to touch the bodies on either side.

Sweat poured from his skin. Sweat against sweat. Thigh against thigh. The dry air singed the lining of his nose, his eyes.

White Buffalo entered through the low doorway, saying the sacred word. "Hey-ya!" he exclaimed, tossing something onto the stones. It sparkled and filled the lodge with the aroma of—sweet grass, herbs, pine? Julio didn't know. Then White Buffalo said something in conversational tones, and the men laughed. Julio wondered whether the laughter was directed at him.

The feeling in the lodge changed. White Buffalo began what Julio believed to be a prayer, earnest, solemn, ending with the familiar word "Ha ho." Everyone echoed, "Ha ho." Then White Buffalo called outside. The two fire tenders lowered the flap, covering the light, shutting out air. Julio strained for a pinpoint of sky through the hides, but there was none. In the darkness the heat forced his eyes to close.

Tzzz! Water! Drops of water sizzled on the hot stones. Steam swirled around his limbs, searing the tissue inside his nostrils. "Ay, Dios!" he gasped. "This is unbearable!"

"Julio!" Dancing Feather's voice eased his panic. "Breathe through this!" Julio felt Dancing Feather's hand touching the sage, lifting it to his face.

"Gracias," he whispered as much to the spirit of the sage as to Dancing Feather, as he breathed through the filtering softness.

Water trickled off his body, down the ridges of his brow. He shivered as the chanting began. First one and then another joined in the "Hey-ya hey-ya, hey-ya hey-ya" rising and swelling, each voice in a different tone. The rhythm pounded against his ears. Soon, without knowing their meaning, Julio found himself drawn into the chanted sounds. "Hey-ya hey-ya, hey-ya hey-ya." Louder and louder he chanted, his body swaying.

Tzzz! More water. More steam. Single outcries pierced the beat. Julio chanted and chanted, inhaling through sage, tasting sage on his lips, feeling bits of sage in his mouth, breathing sage as if the sage and the chant were his only lifelines back through the infernal heat to life.

The chanting came faster. Cries sliced the darkness.

The heat increased. As if something wild inside had been set loose, Julio's frenzy grew. *I can't stand this! Got to get out! Out! The word! What's the word?* He couldn't remember it. He licked his lips, which were distended, swollen. "Dancing Feather!" Over the cries, over the chant, he couldn't be heard. Only the certain pain of stepping on the hot rocks kept him from bolting.

At the loudest peak of wild cries and chanting, all voices stopped, as if by plan. Urgently White Buffalo called out. The fire tenders raised the flap. Julio gasped in the cool, fresh air as it trickled into the lodge. He heard his voice join with the others murmuring, "Ha ho. Ha ho."

He'd made it. He'd done it, whatever it was. He had endured as long as the rest.

A few men began talking, but no one left. "Dancing Feather," Julio whispered. He pointed to the open flap.

Dancing Feather chuckled. "No," he said. Through the dim light Julio could see him point toward the pit. "More."

"More!"

Five more glowing stones were rolled in. One by one they teetered onto the others in the pit, each time threatening burns, each time raising the temperature of the lodge higher than it had been before. Julio shrank away, curling his toes. A water gourd was passed, he sipped, and passed it on. Then the flap was closed again.

The chanting resumed. This time it was different. Not

only the sound but the feeling within the lodge changed. Was it a different spirit? Is that what Dancing Feather would say? With their chanting had they drawn a spirit here? Or two spirits? Somewhere within the circle a drumbeat began, and the men howled like coyotes.

On and on through the night, through the heat, the sound, the steam, the throbbing darkness, each round was hotter, stranger, more difficult than the one before. The ceremony tested Julio to the limit of his endurance. It pushed him. It wrung out his fear and grief until there was nothing left. No feeling. No thoughts. No questions about Papá. Nothing was left but him. Not Mexican, not Cheyenne, not Vé?ho?e, just him, Julio. Not wondering, for once in his life, who he was.

When, after the fourth round, the flap was opened, Julio crawled out behind Dancing Feather. Purged of thought, purged of emotion, he cared about nothing but being alive. He sprawled on the ground. The cool night air swept over his wet skin. The moon. It was high in the sky. He'd been in the lodge for hours.

His reverie was broken by a startled yelp from the stream. It was followed by another and the sound of splashing water and laughter.

"Come on," Dancing Feather said, swaying above him, he, too, still recovering from the heat.

"No." Julio returned his gaze to the moon.

"Yes. It's important" Dancing Feather prodded him

with his toe.

The cold water of the stream felt like a thousand tiny arrows. Shouting, whooping, tingling all over, he leapt from the stream, Dancing Feather fast behind him. Laughing and shivering, Julio scrambled into his pants, but his laughter stopped when he saw the strange way Dancing Feather was looking at him. "Now you are Tse-tséhésé," he said.

Dancing Feather turned to his father and the other Tse-tséhésé. He said in Spanish, then in Cheyenne, "We are brothers."

Chapter Sixteen

Julio ambled through the moonlit night back toward camp. Nothing seemed real. The black trees—were they shadows of themselves, or were they images of moonlight pretending to be trees? An owl hooted low from a glowing limb. Another higher pitched hoot answered. Julio did not make the sign of the cross.

Peace. He had never before felt such tranquility. Everything he smelled and heard seemed as if it stood alone as the most important event in the universe. The air was sweet, clean.

He was drifting more than walking. He had become a part of the earth, of the twigs crunching beneath his moccasins and the swish and scent of the grass. He had become one with the Cheyenne. Even more, with life.

The ground shuddered ever so slightly beneath his feet, and Julio heard a sound like distant thunder. Everyone stopped. Then, as if suddenly awakened, time raced forward. Women from the camp galloped on horseback through the cottonwoods, yelling.

Julio ran to Dancing Feather's side. "What is it? What's happening?"

"Buffalo! Buffalo are running. The old ones have already killed two near our village." Riders were jumping down from their mounts, thrusting quivers and arrows into the young men's outstretched hands.

Riding a spotted horse, leading another, Silent Walker zigzagged through the melee. Julio jumped back to avoid being trampled. The horses pranced and nickered, pricking their ears toward the distant rumble. Silent Walker's eyes flashed in the moonlight as she gestured that one horse was for Dancing Feather, one for him.

Horses were whinnying and stamping everywhere. The hot, dusty flank of Silent Walker's horse jostled against him as she slid down. Dancing Feather mounted, pulling his arrow and quiver over his head. "Great Buffalo Spirit has heard our call!" He reined the horse, pivoted, and darted from the trees with a loud cry, never looking back.

As abruptly as the area had filled, it emptied of men and horses. Only the women, one black horse, and Julio remained. In all his life he had never felt so ashamed.

What would his Tse-tséhésé brothers think of him now? He did not know how to ride a horse.

A great feast followed the hunt. The men ate pieces of liver, still warm, sprinkled with gall. Women cooked steaks and tripe and tongue, and Julio gorged himself on the tender buffalo meat, eating until he could eat no more. Chivita and the other dogs and then the coyotes and wolves had their fill.

But since the ceremony in the sweat lodge, Dancing Feather had avoided him. Maybe it was only because there had been much work to do. All the meat had to be cut and carried back to the camp, sliced into thin strips and hung to dry, or cooked before it spoiled. Hides were scraped and treated for making clothing, tipis, and rawhide rope. Horns and bones were carved into tools and ladles. And stomachs were cleaned to use as cooking bags. Little of the buffalo was wasted.

Julio slumped against a fallen cottonwood, picking burrs from Chivita's coat, feeling left out and useless. Singlehanded he could take care of himself and his flock. He could use a sling as well as any grown man in Taos. He had survived alone in the wilderness. Whatever he did, he was used to doing very well. But here...even the youngest Tse-tséhésé children rode as if they'd been born on horseback. How could he ever explain to Dancing Feather and White Buffalo that he could not?

Thump! Thump! Two pebbles bounced against his shirt. Silent Walker was kneeling by a huge buffalo hide. Her scraping tool lay before her. She pointed, and Julio's eyes followed. White Buffalo and Dancing Feather were walking in a direct path toward him.

Julio stood up. He tried to swallow.

White Buffalo stopped. Dancing Feather's face was like a painted mask. In his strong voice White Buffalo greeted Julio in Cheyenne, then gestured for him to sit down.

When they were sitting cross-legged in the dirt, White Buffalo peered far into the distance. "A half moon ago the Tse-tsėhésė found a boy, blind, dying on the trail. A brave boy. We cared for this boy. We carried him on a travois, treated his eyes and his wounds. We gave him moccasins, food. We honored him in the lodge as the Tse-tsėhésė honor brave young men." White Buffalo's eyes turned to Julio. "Has this young warrior lost his honor, that he refuses to hunt buffalo? Has he become a child again, to stay behind in the camp with the children?"

Julio chose his words carefully. "White Buffalo, it is true. The Tse-tsėhésė have been good to me. I want to kill buffalo for the tribe, for food and tipis and moccasins. I want to repay your kindness. But first I must learn how to ride a horse."

The dark pits in Dancing Feather's eyes lightened with understanding.

"In Taos," Julio went on, "only the rich have horses. My family is poor. I do not know how to ride."

It was as if a kettle had splashed into the flames. Words and phrases in Spanish, English, and Cheyenne spewed together, and the stiff faces relaxed into smiles. White Buffalo rose to his feet, laughing and shaking his head. Gesturing toward the south, he spoke to Dancing Feather in Cheyenne. His tone was solemn, as when he had spoken in the lodge. "Dancing Feather will tell you." He turned and walked away.

Julio blinked. "What?" He turned to Dancing Feather. "What will you tell me?"

"How to trap eagles."

"Eagles!" What did eagles have to do with—with anything?

With a tilt of his chin Dancing Feather indicated south, the direction in which White Buffalo had pointed. "In the canyons you will trap eagles. You trade eagle feathers for a horse. Then you learn to ride." Dancing Feather took a deep breath. "With Tse-tsėhėsė you will not be poor. You will ride like a warrior."

Julio's ears buzzed. Own a horse? His own horse? Ride like the Cheyenne? A stone stung his cheek.

"Hey!" Spinning around, he yelled at Silent Walker. "Would you quit that?"

Silent Walker's eyes were sparkling, and she pointed west.

"Dancing Feather, tell her! If she wants to get my attention, just say something."

"She doesn't speak—"

"I know she doesn't speak Spanish! Just tell her to talk to me in Cheyenne. I'll learn."

"Silent Walker doesn't speak Cheyenne. She doesn't speak anything. Ever. She can't."

"She can't?"

Thump! Thump! Two more pebbles bounced against Julio's shirt. At his feet Chivita's head jerked up, her ears pricked forward.

Silent Walker's hands were making circles in the air, around and around and around. Then she pointed again.

First all he saw was a cloud of dust; then, as the cloud drew nearer, he could see wagons and people and hear the bleating of sheep. Wagons. Mexican wagons from home!

Taos life was like a dream from long ago. But wagons were coming from that life to this—wagons going to Bent's Fort.

Chapter Seventeen

The wagons ground past with nods and waves from their drivers. The Cheyenne waved back. Children ran alongside the wagons. Young men galloped bareback, calling their greetings. Only the wagon master and two other men stopped to talk with White Buffalo and the tribal elders.

Julio wanted to listen, but he had to chase after Chivita, who was already hard at work doing what she'd been trained to do—herd sheep. Her head low to the ground, she was circling behind the stragglers to keep them together. "Chivita! No! No! This isn't our flock. Chivita, come here!"

Reluctantly she came, tongue lolling, and dropped at Julio's side. "Good girl, Chivita. You miss the sheep, don't you?" Julio thrust his hand deep into the lanolin-rich wool of a passing ewe.

"Ah! ¡Qué buena perrita! What a good dog!" The sheep herder brought up the tail of the caravan, eating dust. "Don't suppose you'd want to trade her for a few sheep." Walking toward him, the shepherd took off his wide-brimmed hat and flicked off some of the dust. His face was two-toned, light above and dark below the brim line, the creases blackened with dirt.

Julio stepped closer, blinking. "Helacio?"

The man stopped dead in his tracks. "¡Ay! ¡Santa María, Madre de Dios!" he exclaimed. "Julio? Is that you?"

Julio nodded.

"¡Ay, Dios! B–but—" Helacio glanced toward the Cheyenne village and back to Julio. "I thought you were at the fort with your Papá. I have brought something for him. Is *he* here too?"

The jostling river of dusty white wool blurred before Julio's eyes. He shook his head, couldn't speak.

Julio was engulfed in Helacio's dusty arms, pressed into his big barrel chest and the smell of his sweat. Julio's knees buckled beneath him.

Finally Julio wiped his nose and stood on his own. "Papá?...He didn't have a chance, Helacio." He wiped his eyes on the backs of his hands. "I—I didn't...Seeing you made it so real again."

"Julio, when? What happened?"

"On our third night out. Apaches."

Helacio turned away. Looking back toward the mountains, he crossed himself and stood silently, shaking his head. "Enrique was a good man." He stared westward again, wiping his nose. "You...! You haven't even reached Bent's Fort yet!" Helacio exclaimed. "Where...? How did you...?"

"Eh! Eh! Helacio!" the wagon master yelled. "Wake up! Get it moving!" The wagon train had moved on. Sheep were scattered here and there, browsing on the prairie stubble.

Julio signaled to Chivita. Barking, she sprang into action.

Julio stepped into stride beside Helacio, walking briskly. "You come on with us, Julio. The fort's only another couple of days away. You can join up there with the next Taos-bound wagons and go back home to your family."

A pebble whapped against Julio's leg. Julio pivoted in the direction from which it had come. Silent Walker was standing with Dancing Feather beneath a cottonwood, making a face, shaking her head no, pointing back to the tipis. Dancing Feather's arms were crossed over his chest. His expression was masked.

"I—" Julio hesitated. "I don't know, Helacio. The Cheyenne...They've been good to me."

"Julio!" Helacio stopped so abruptly, Julio thought he had stumbled. "You don't belong with them. They're not your people!"

"Who are my people, Helacio?"

Helacio paused. He put his hand on Julio's shoulder and sighed. "I don't know. Your Papá never told you?"

Julio shook his head. "He would have, I think, the night he was..."

"Enrique loved you as much as any blood son. That never made any difference to him. Julio, you know that."

"I know." Julio pushed the toe of his moccasin through the dirt. "But I've known for a long time I was...different." Julio glanced once again toward the trees. "Helacio, I'll see you at the fort. I can't leave the Cheyenne. We'll get to the fort soon enough."

Helacio rubbed his hand across the stubble on his face. "You're making a mistake, Julio."

"I don't think so."

"Take care of that dog. She's too good a sheep dog to let them boil her for stew." Still shaking his head, Helacio resumed his pace behind the flock. Julio watched him move away. *Is Helacio right? Am I making a mistake?* "Helacio!" He broke into a run. "You said you had something—for Papá. Could I...?"

"Pah! I forgot! We'll have to catch up with the wagons."

Running, they overtook the last wagon. Helacio crawled inside, pawing through packages and canvas bags, and lifted one out.

The bundle was tied with twine. The outside layer was a heavy wool shirt that had hung from a hook above Papá's sleeping mat in the little adobe house. Julio drew it to his nose and inhaled, hoping.

"It's from your Mamá. She said"—Helacio rubbed his ear—"your father might need it."

Julio stiffened. "He won't." He hugged the bundle to his chest.

"And she said *you* might need what's inside."

"Did—did she send any other message for me?"

"Nothing more than that." Helacio looked away. Julio could see the muscles in his neck as he swallowed. "Life's not easy, is it?" Helacio rubbed his ear again. "Sometimes we just have to make the best of these things and go on."

"That's what I'm going to do."

Helacio nodded. "Is there anything you need, Julio?" He was repacking the load in the wagon where Papá's bundle had been.

"No," Julio said, then remembered. "Oh, yes! There is. Could you take this to Mr. Bent? Papá was carrying it to him." He pulled the paper from his leather bag and handed it to Helacio, averting his eyes from the stain.

Helacio crossed himself, then tucked the letter into his gear. "Anything else?"

"Well, yes, there is. Helacio, could you spare some coffee beans?"

"Coffee beans?" Helacio laughed. "For you we could!"

He rummaged in the wagon again and tossed Julio a burlap bag.

Julio waited until all the sheep had passed, then called Chivita and walked back to the Cheyenne camp. The *shu—shu—shu* of sharp-edged rocks scraping hides sounded like the hiss of escaping steam as he wove his way among tipis and racks of drying buffalo jerky, where the Cheyenne women were still working. He didn't see Dancing Feather anywhere, but Silent Walker was kneeling beside a huge buffalo hide. She looked up, and her eyes opened wide. Her face broke into an animated smile. Julio knew, even without her gestures, she'd thought he'd gone with the wagons.

Tucking the burlap bag of coffee beans under his arm against Papá's shirt, he scooped up a pebble from the ground and tossed it at her. "Nobody there to throw rocks at me!" he said, shaking his head. "It would have been boring. No eagles to trap. No horses."

Silent Walker stuck out her bottom lip and twisted her face into a frown.

"So you don't understand me. Hey, if I can learn Cheyenne, you can learn Spanish—at least to listen to it." But, sorry for her confusion, he pointed to himself, saying, "Julio, Tse-tsėhésė," then to the ground—"I'm staying here"—then to her—"with you."

That she understood. The other women did, too, and smiled over their labors. The *shu—shu—shu* sounds stopped. He could feel all eyes watching him as he stepped through the maze to a weathered hide spread, fur down, on the ground. On the hide sat a fresh buffalo head, upside down, balanced on the tips of the horns, brains exposed. Nearby lay a pile of fat. Néške?e was humming as she pounded the brains and fat together on a rectangular stone.

"Néške?e!"

"Ho!" Néške?e reared back, threw up her arms, and began to jabber, pointing toward the trail, the wagons, him, the trail eastward, herself. He thought she was scolding him for making her think he'd gone away without saying good-bye. He glanced over his shoulder at Silent Walker. She was doubled over with silent laughter, her braids jiggling against her shoulders.

"Néške?e, Néške?e!" He slid the bag of coffee into the palm of his hand, cradling it like a ball. "No, Néške?e. I'm still here. And I have coffee. For you. Mo?ȯhtavė-hohpe," he said, raising the bag and smiling. "From me"—he touched the coffee to his chest—"to you. E-peva?e." Then he touched his eyes.

Chapter Eighteen

"Dancing Feather! How do I trap eagles? I would be honored if you would teach me the Tse-tsėhésė way."

Dancing Feather smiled. Really smiled. The next day they were on their way.

Dancing Feather adjusted the load on Julio's back, jerking him off balance. Over his shoulder Julio could smell the willow basket, like the smell of the riverside. Inside were leather gloves, hand stitched with the same tiny stitches as his moccasins, and something round and white, but he couldn't tell what it was. His knife hung in the sheath at his waist, and, as always, he carried the leather bag with Teresita's stone.

As they walked Dancing Feather said, "Blue Cloud Woman is happy with the coffee. She hopes you get many feathers."

"Blue Cloud Woman?" Julio asked. "Who's that?" "Néške⁊e."

"Dancing Feather! You're talking in riddles. Néške⁊e can't have two names."

"In Cheyenne," Dancing Feather said, *"Néške⁊e* means 'grandmother.' Blue Cloud Woman is *my* Néške⁊e, my father's mother." He tapped his chest above the bear claw.

Julio covered his eyes with one hand. *"Néške⁊e* means 'grandmother?' But why didn't you tell me? I've been calling Blue Cloud Woman 'Grandmother' ever since the first time I saw you."

"Néške⁊e likes it when you say 'Grandmother.' Everyone thinks it is funny."

"Well I don't! I don't like people laughing at me." Julio tugged at the straps on the basket, then grinned.

"Anyway, I'm glad Néške⁊e likes the coffee." Chivita sniffed at the basket and looked quizzically at Dancing Feather.

"Néške⁊e took care of me once too," Dancing Feather said. "She saved this arm." He looked down at the arm with the three parallel scars. "I was clawed by a bear."

"A bear!"

Dancing Feather nodded. "This bear." He touched the claw hanging from the leather thong around his neck.

Chivita put her front paws high on Julio's legs.

"No, you can't go to the canyons, Chivita." Julio shook

his head and ruffled the fur behind her ears. "You'd scare away the eagles. We can't even take a packhorse."

As if she understood, Chivita whined and cocked her head. Her big eyes became sad.

"Where's Silent Walker?" Julio asked. It was early, and the camp was still quiet.

"We'll get her now." Dancing Feather slid his bow over his head.

At Silent Walker's tipi Dancing Feather softly called her name. Julio heard movement inside. Sleepy-eyed and yawning, Silent Walker crawled out, her unbraided hair falling loose around her shoulders.

Julio patted his leg. "Chivita," he called. Again Chivita reached her front paws up his thigh. He scratched behind her ears and down her neck, then looked at Silent Walker. "Chivita can't go with us," he said, shaking his head so Silent Walker would understand. "Will you keep her for me?"

Silent Walker put her arms around Chivita and smiled.

Julio looked at Dancing Feather. "But please ask her not to make Chivita carry wood."

Julio and Dancing Feather struck off in a southwesterly direction from the Arkansas River toward shadowy dark lines that hinted of canyons. Julio had expected to travel due west, but this was southwest. This way would not take them toward the mountains but into desolate Mexican territory.

A rabbit darted from under some sage brush, zigzagging a crooked path. He and Dancing Feather froze. Then, like flashes of lightning, two arms shot forward, one releasing an arrow, the other a rock. The rabbit fell. "You shoot fast," Dancing Feather said.

"You do too."

"Don't clean it." Dancing Feather stopped Julio from pulling out his knife. "The rabbit will bring eagles."

Dancing Feather dropped the rabbit into the basket on Julio's back. The sun blazed down. It was hot and getting hotter. With luck they wouldn't have to go too far. Julio hoped they would find shade soon.

"Julio, stop!"

A few feet before them lay the ragged edge of a canyon, so unexpected and so steep he could have fallen over the rim unaware. The sun had eased to the west, and Julio realized they had been walking a long time. He could smell the rabbit in the basket on his back.

"Thanks," Julio said slowly, licking his dry lips. Not eating had affected him. This hunt would be done the Cheyenne way, fasting until after the eagles were trapped, and it had already been a long time since they had eaten or drunk anything.

The canyon, cut into the flat plain, seemed an impossibility, like a dream rather than an actual place. Julio and Dancing Feather wandered along the rim, searching for a spot for the eagle trap. "Eagles soar on the wind rising up from the canyons," Dancing Feather said. "They nest on these rims.

"We dig a hole and cover it with a lid of woven branches. Then we put the rabbit on the lid as bait and hide inside the hole."

On a rocky ledge at the top of the canyon, they discovered a round opening that sank deep inside the rock, like a shaft.

"Dancing Feather!" Julio peered inside. "This is it! This is the place."

Dancing Feather frowned. "No. We always dig a hole in the earth."

"But don't you see?" Julio said. "The Earth Mother has already done our work for us. We can cover the top of *this* hole."

Dancing Feather stood, looking thoughtfully at the hole in the rock, then nodded, but not without adding, "The Tse-tsėhésė way is to dig a hole with sticks. It takes four days."

Four days!

But Dancing Feather at last agreed on the site for the trap, and he and Julio began to inch down the canyon wall, scuttling loose rock down the steep sides.

At the bottom of the canyon Julio scanned the rocks, which reflected the canyon in miniature, striped with the colors of yellow dust, brown earth, and red clay. He and Dancing Feather were not the first to see this place. Chipped into the rock were pictures—antelope running, a double sun with rays, corn, and symbols Julio did not understand, like a crooked line that could have been a snake or a river and a circle with a mark running through the top and out the bottom.

Gigantic petrified mudballs clustered on the floor of the canyon. Seams protruded from these ancient rocks like veins in an old man's hand, and rays of sun glimmered from the hard, milky crystals exposed in the mudballs that had cracked open.

Julio wanted to select some crystals for his sisters, but Dancing Feather was calling.

"Julio, come on. Let's get to work." He motioned toward the dry riverbed in the belly of the canyon. Earlier in the spring it had carried runoff from the mountains, but now it was dry, an arroyo. Julio picked up a few crystals, put them in his bag, then followed.

"We have to gather wood for the trap and lodge and for our fire," Dancing Feather said, already heading for a scraggly half-dead cottonwood on the sandy banks of the arroyo. He climbed up the large trunk and began breaking off leafy limbs. Julio gathered weathered cedar branches long enough to make a grid across the hole and strong enough to support the rabbit's weight. They would weave the lid tomorrow.

Without consulting Dancing Feather he scraped a hollow

in the damp sand in the arroyo and lined the hole with a piece of leather. Either by seepage or by condensation water would collect there during the night. He knew there would be no drinking it until the eagles were trapped, but sooner or later they would have to have water. Julio licked his cracked lips and tried not to think how long that might be. Hunger had passed. The thirst was endless.

"Julio!" Dancing Feather jumped down from the tree, pointing to the limbs he had broken from the cottonwood. "Let's take these for the lodge." When the wood had been moved, they began to prepare for morning. They carried rocks and wood, selected the sacred sage, laid a fire, and constructed a lean-to covered with branches and sarapes for the lodge. Julio watched as Dancing Feather took some tobacco from the leather pouch. He made ten small bundles, then hung them on sticks which he stuck into the ground behind the fire circle. "Don't touch them," Dancing Feather said.

On the fire Dancing Feather sprinkled sweet grass. As it burned, they rubbed the smoke onto their bodies. Then Dancing Feather lifted his arms to the slice of red evening sky above the rim of the canyon and began to sing. The song echoed eerily up and down the canyon walls. Into the night he sang, bowing, bending, lifting his arms and shoulders in heavy flight, casting strange eagle-shaped shadows on the rose-hued canyon walls until Julio fell asleep.

He dreamed of eagles.

In the predawn darkness mourning doves cooed. Julio awoke thinking he was home in Mamá's house, doves cooing in the mesquite outside, but he opened his eyes to black canyon walls and remembered where he was—and why. It was strange, mourning doves living here on this hot, uninhabited plain.

He sat up, brushed away the sand that clung to his body, and swung his bag over his shoulder. "Dancing Feather," he said, waking him. "It's time."

Dancing Feather sprang to his feet. He slid the bear claw into place in the middle of his chest, raised his arms to the gray sky, and offered an invocation. He leaned toward the wood, flint in hand, to start the fire they had laid last night. That's when Julio heard the buzz. Faster than he could think, before he had spotted the source, his sling was whirling circles in the air by his ear.

"Don't move!" he yelled. The stone ripped past Dancing Feather into the intertwined branches beside him, and the rattling stopped.

Dancing Feather, eyes wide, raked a diamondback with seven rattles out from the brush. "Ha ho." His voice was barely audible. Dancing Feather stood a moment without speaking, then walked away.

Julio bent down and cut off the rattles and dropped them into his bag with Teresita's stone.

The fire flamed and burned down, flamed again and

burned down. Shadows ceased dancing on the canyon's walls. Julio brought the water that had collected in the leather pouch during the night, yearning to wet his dry lips and tongue instead of sprinkling the water on hot stones.

When the rocks were hot and glowing, both he and Dancing Feather rolled them into the pit in their lean-to. They went in, and Dancing Feather closed the flaps.

Dancing Feather chanted, then was silent. A feeling of reverence settled around them, just as it had when White Buffalo had led the ceremony. Julio had wondered if it would be the same without him. Even in the heat he shivered.

"Hey—ya...!" The chanting began...

Heat...

chanting...sage

stones...steam...sweat...heat

chanting...

swirling...

spirits...

After the fourth round, Julio and Dancing Feather stumbled out into the dawn, cleansed, ready to call forth the sacred bird of the sun.

Chapter Nineteen

"Vermilion," Dancing Feather said when he reached into the basket. He set a red-stained gourd on a stone. "Mixed with eagle fat, a gift from White Buffalo." Dancing Feather smeared a swipe of red grease over his chest, then leaned toward Julio. One whiff and Julio knew what it was for— to disguise his human scent with the eagle smell.

After Dancing Feather finished streaking Julio's face, Julio did the same for him, then rubbed the rest of the mixture across his own chest. Chivita wasn't the only one to have fattened up since they had been with the Cheyenne. The rich buffalo meats had been good for them both.

"Sage," Dancing Feather said, jerking Julio's focus back to the present. The lack of food and water was making it hard for him to concentrate. "Basket. Leather ties. Branches. Gloves."

Julio picked up the cedar and cottonwood branches they would use to build a lid for the trap. He picked up an arrow-shaped stone, too, for protection, just in case. Dancing Feather carried the rest. They left their clothes and everything else they didn't need in the canyon.

As they climbed, Julio's light-headedness made him feel he was in flight. Like the eagle, he soared up and out of the canyon, spiraling higher and higher above the earth until everything below became small. He looked back down and saw Dancing Feather, tiny as a stinging red ant, disappear altogether.

In spite of the bright morning sky there was a sense of unreality about what they were doing. They staggered up onto the rim of the canyon and deposited their loads. Julio broke off fresh sage branches, swung his legs over the edge of the hole, and jumped inside. As he spread the sweet sage on the floor, he found himself thinking of the hole as a cave and realized that, like a rock cave, this would be cooler than a dirt hole would have been.

"This isn't good," Dancing Feather grunted, leaning over and peering into the hole. "There's no dirt to stake the rabbit."

"Will *that* work?" Julio tried not to smile as he pointed to his rock and a leather thong. He did smile, and his lip cracked and bled.

Dancing Feather tested the weight of the rock and answered only with "Huh."

Tying the thong first onto the rock, then onto the bait, Julio was glad the rabbit would be above them and not in the hole. It was ripe.

Dancing Feather handed down the basket, which Julio pushed to the side of the hole. Then together, one above, one below, they wove the cedar and cottonwood branches across the top, leaving an opening. Dancing Feather dropped through the opening, cradling a human skull in his arm.

Julio jerked away. His hand automatically made the sign of the cross. "Why that?" he stammered.

"It will protect us from the eagle's talons. It will make the eagle as blind as you were, so he can't see us." Dancing Feather nodded solemnly, rubbing the white top of the skull. "And it will keep you awake."

Julio had not been worried about falling asleep before, but he knew he wouldn't sleep now, not with that in here with him. He wondered who it was. Or whose it was. Had he—or she?—been Cheyenne? Mexican? Kiowa? American? Whoever it was, its purpose had not been to make two eagle trappers invisible.

Julio thrust the rabbit up through the opening in the center of the branches, testing the thong to be sure it would withstand the dive of an eagle. Dancing Feather camouflaged the opening with more cottonwood and cedar.

"We can't see out." Julio leaned his head back and to the side. The spots of blue and sunlight shimmering through the leaves weren't large enough to see an eagle in the sky. "How—"

"The eagle will come fast. Listen." Dancing Feather handed Julio the pair of gloves but left his own hands bare. *A concession because I'm not Cheyenne*, Julio thought, but he slipped his hands into the leather.

"Now, don't talk. Talk only to the Eagle Spirit."

It seemed to Julio that as Dancing Feather hunkered down, he went away. Julio could almost see him soaring up and out across the plain, and he tried to do the same.

He imagined the great bird, the golden eagle, gliding gracefully from a crag, leaving a huge nest with two or three hungry eaglets—but then he stopped that image. He was going to trap this eagle. Let it be without hungry young. Let it be a young male, like himself, free in the world.

He began to imagine again. He had nearly killed an eagle once. With lightning speed it had swooped down on a lamb and grabbed it in its talons. The poor lamb was bleating, its feet already off the ground before Julio could send a rock flying from his sling. The stone only grazed the eagle, but it dropped the lamb, then swooped above Julio's head, wings spread wide, momentarily blocking off the sun. He had never before realized how large an eagle was. Thinking again of it, he remembered every detail— the light undersides of the arching talons, the feathers that grew like fringed chaps to the toes, the beak that was nearly as long as the head. From the tip of one wing to the tip of the other was the length of the diamondback rattler in the brush this morning.

Julio's legs were cramped. The rock hole was stuffy and hot. He was thirsty. Unintentionally jostling Dancing Feather, Julio shifted, wondering how long they had been in there when, like wind shooting through a funnel of rock, the sound came.

He tensed. Dancing Feather's muscles quivered; he raised his hands, fingers spread, eyes flashing.

Tzuuuu! Whump! Traveling at the speed of an arrow, the eagle seized the rabbit. The stone shot up from the floor, smashing against Julio's shin. He grabbed the thong; his feet jerked up from the floor.

The eagle let go. As Julio staggered against the cave wall, he heard the labored pumping of the mighty wings lifting away.

His disappointment—though he would not want to admit it to Dancing Feather—was mixed with relief. How could the two of them, strong as they were, wrestle this mighty bird?

Tzuuuu! Whump! Whump! This time the eagle landed. The trap darkened under the shadow of its body. Its feathers rustled, and it cried a loud, shrill call before it tore into the rabbit.

Dancing Feather glanced at Julio, eyebrows raised. Trailing the thong, his bare hands reached up toward the hole, closer, closer, within a finger's length of the eagle's talons. Julio held his breath. Then, like a striking viper, Dancing Feather's arms shot through the branches.

"Ay!" Dancing Feather yelled. The eagle screeched. Branches and limbs and feathers flew everywhere. The great wings beat with the strength of horses' legs. Black eyes blazed with fury.

"Julio! Pull some feathers! Quick!"

Julio reached toward the flared tail feathers, but the beak streaked downward, striking his gloves, hitting his skin. The legs in Dancing Feather's grasp jerked him this way and that. The talons raked Dancing Feather's chest and face—drawing blood.

"Hurry, Julio," he cried.

Julio lunged. Dancing Feather had managed to pull the eagle deep into the hole. It was thrashing more violently than ever, the golden brown of the neck and head flashing in the sun, beak slashing. Dancing Feather struggled to wrap the thong around its legs, but even bound together, they continued to pump as the great bird screeched in rage. Julio seized a feather from the tail and tugged. The eagle screamed. "Ho!" Julio said as the feather tore loose.

"Fast, Julio. More!"

The bird was panting, tongue arching and falling. Black eyes flashed red. Dodging the head, Julio pulled another feather from the opposite side: to balance the damage. This time he was not gentle. Then using both hands, he pulled on the tail as hard as he could. "Ha ho, great eagle," Julio said aloud, clutching a handful of feathers. "I am sorry. No more!" he yelled at Dancing Feather. "Let him go!"

Dancing Feather ripped the thong from the talons and heaved the eagle upward, releasing it. The eagle flapped and stumbled through the scattered branches, then lifted off.

Neither Julio nor Dancing Feather moved. They were both panting, perspiring heavily. Julio wiped the back of his hand across his forehead. After the sweat lodge and long thirst he could not imagine where sweat could be coming from. He was beginning to feel his wounds. There were many. Blood trickled down his arms and chest from the pecks and lacerations, and bruises were forming where the wings had landed. There was an ugly knot on his leg from the stone.

Dancing Feather had been beaten and scratched even worse. His cheek was gouged, and blood dripped from his chin.

As if with one breath, both Dancing Feather and Julio sighed and leaned against the wall. Their eyes met. They had worked well together, as if of one mind. Julio reached out. Dancing Feather's hands closed around his in a clasp that was strong, binding more than flesh to flesh. Binding even more deeply, spirit to spirit. It was *this* he had missed with sisters, *this* he had missed with Papá.

"The Eagle Spirit is good to you, Julio. Let's rebuild the

trap. More eagles will come."

"No!"

Dancing Feather looked confused. "But Julio, the Eagle Spirit answered. We will get many feathers."

"No!" Julio repeated, cutting him off. "No. We will not trap more eagles. We have enough feathers. Enough for me, and for you. These are enough."

Dancing Feather was quiet. Gradually his breathing slowed, and a smile spread across his bloodstained face. "Julio, you have the spirit of the eagle inside you," he said. "You respect the eagle. Julio, you and the eagle are brothers. Now you are a true Tse-tsêhésê! You have found your Cheyenne name—Soaring Eagle." Dancing Feather nodded, standing proudly. "Soaring Eagle. This is very good. Silent Walker walks on the earth, Soaring Eagle soars in the sky."

"Soaring Eagle..." The words rasped across Julio's dry lips. He *was* a soaring eagle; he had flown from his cage, and he belonged where he had landed.

Dancing Feather raised his hands to the back of his neck, pulled his leather necklace over his head, and held it in front of him. "Soaring Eagle, this is for you." He hung it around Julio's neck.

Julio stared at the bear claw curving against his skin. "Ha ho, Dancing Feather. Ha ho." There could be only one greater gift, and that, Dancing Feather had already given—the gift of friendship.

Chapter Twenty

"You lost!" Julio opened his right hand, showing nothing inside, then opened the left, where the pebble nestled in the cup of his palm.

"Humpf!" Dancing Feather tossed Julio his last feather. It was a Cheyenne game, but Julio had outguessed Dancing Feather almost every time.

"No!" Laughing, Julio handed back the feathers. "It's only a game, and I don't want your feathers. Keep them for a horse of your own." Then, as Dancing Feather hesitated, he convinced him by adding, "Without you I wouldn't have feathers *or* a horse, would I?"

Dancing Feather nodded as he reached for the feathers, but the jovial mood of the evening had changed. They had feasted on a small antelope Julio had killed with his sling.

They saved the tiny horns and hoofs for Néške?e, and the soft skin for Silent Walker. Coyotes were now feasting and growling over the carcass he and Dancing Feather could not use.

A fire crackled before them, and as Dancing Feather stood gazing into it, his troubled face glowed in the light. Julio had seen that look, on the trail when Dancing Feather had talked about trapping eagles with his father, and several times before. It had always seemed to emerge from some private pain, some worry deep inside.

"This is not a good time for the Tse-tséhésé," Dancing Feather said slowly, hunkering down beside the fire. "The power of the Cheyenne is gone." He gazed into the fire.

Afraid that any response might stop Dancing Feather from saying more, Julio waited.

"When Bent's Fort was built, stars fell from the sky." Dancing Feather poked a stick into the embers, stirring sparks. "The Tse-tséhésé thought the world was dying. They thought it was the final battle between earth and sky. They painted their bodies and their horses. All night they rode around the fort, shaking their spears and bows. No Cheyenne died then. There was no death with honor. Now the Cheyenne nation is dying little by little like an old man."

"But, Dancing Feather, Papá told me the Cheyenne are a great nation—"

"Many people have come. White people and white people with black skin—Americans, Frenchmen, Texans.

Before, there were great herds of buffalo. Now, sometimes the Tse-tsėhésė go hungry. White men kill the buffalo. Kill the beaver. Kill the grass. Kill the cottonwoods. They bring sickness and whiskey. Tse-tsėhésė, Paiute, and many from other tribes die the sick death of white men. Not the death with honor, not the death of a warrior." He sprang to his feet with an anguished cry, raised his arms, and began to dance and chant.

Julio shuddered. Dancing Feather's chant was in Cheyenne, and though Julio did not know the words, he understood. The gestures were violent—the thrust of the spear, the stab of the knife, the shooting of the arrow. Julio shook his head. Dancing Feather was pleading with the Great Spirit. "Santa María," Julio prayed silently, "help me understand. How can a people feel the spirit of God in the sage and eagle and still want to kill each other to die what they call honorable deaths in battle?"

Dancing Feather sank to the ground by the embers of the fire. In a deep monotone he said, "Nothing lives long, only the earth and the mountains."

The fire flared. Distorted shadows danced on the canyon walls and rustled in the dry grass. Julio's thoughts wandered back to the eagle. The quest for eagle feathers, he realized, had to do with more than feathers and horses.

The silver streaks in Dancing Feather's unbraided hair reflected the firelight. Dancing Feather leaned forward. "Soaring Eagle," he said without looking up, "when the

Mexican wagon train passed, I thought you went with them. Why didn't you?"

Julio lifted the bear claw between his thumb and forefinger, scraping his nail back and forth against the sharp curve. *Why didn't I?* It wasn't an easy question. "When I left Taos with Papá," he said, "I wanted to make adobe bricks at Bent's Fort with him. After he died, I wanted to get there to find a priest, a holy man, to—" He waved the rest of the sentence away. How could he possibly explain all that to Dancing Feather? "I didn't go on with Papá's old friend because—Well, because of you, and Silent Walker and Néškeʔe. Because Tse-tséhésé life is good."

"And when we arrive at Bent's Fort...?" Dancing Feather still did not look up.

Julio took a deep breath. "I don't know." He pressed the bear claw against his chest. "After the sweat lodge you said I was not Mexican. You said I was Tse-tséhésé. Who am I, Dancing Feather?" The words blurted out too hard, too fast.

"You are Tse-tséhésé. You are Soaring Eagle."

"But before?"

"You were Mexican. Before, maybe you were born English or American or French. You look like that. But now you are Soaring Eagle. Before Silent Walker was Tse-tséhésé, she was born Kiowa." Dancing Feather stood, and his voice became deep like White Buffalo's. "Why is it important? Now is what is important. Soaring Eagle, the

Tse-tsėhésė way to know a path is to ask for a dream. We seek a vision. Each one goes alone." He gestured upward, then downward with his hand. "We go to the mountain or to the canyon until the Great Spirit gives a sign."

Julio let his eyes travel up the orange and black canyon shadows. Lonely, isolated, it was, nevertheless, a place that called to him. He liked it here. *And if I am to be Tse-tsėhésė... What would happen if I stayed? If I had a vision, would my future become clear?* "Dancing Feather, how do you find this vision?"

"Alone. No food. No water. For four days you wait. You listen. When you know, you will know." Dancing Feather began to sprinkle water on the coals. "When you return, White Buffalo will interpret what you see." Still holding the stick he had used for stirring the coals, Dancing Feather stood and raised his arms.

"Great Spirit, Grandfather, all powers of the world; spirits of air, fire, earth, and water; spirits of north, south, east, and west; all powers that move above and below; spirits of stars, moon, sun, and light; spirits of the grasses and rivers and trees of our Grandmother; all animal brothers, and sisters of rivers and seas, all sacred peoples of the earth: Listen! This young man is calling to you, Grandmother. He is asking for a sacred relationship with you. He is seeking a vision of who he is to be."

The next morning when Julio awoke, Dancing Feather had gone.

Chapter Twenty-One

Until the third day nothing happened. Heat, thirst,
hunger. Loneliness. Julio never moved far from the place
where he and Dancing Feather had slept.

On the third day he found his eyes drooping closed,
yet he thought he was awake. There was a buzzing in his
ears, like distant locusts. The walls of the canyon seemed
to accordion in and out, in and out, shimmering in the sun.
The buzz, too, went in and out. In and out. Louder, fainter,
then louder again. Hour after hour, sun low, sun high.
Finally, as the sun passed the zenith, through the sound, so
faintly he had to lean forward to capture it, came a tune.

It was like the song of his flute in the night, but it was the
solitary voice of a woman. He did not open his eyes. He
knew she wasn't there, but he leaned forward and let the

sweet, sad tones fill him with an indescribable yearning. He began to distinguish words.

"…cherry…no stone…

…love a chicken…bone

…my love a ring without no end…"

He listened, entranced. His voice was hoarse, but he began to hum the melody. Later the words came too. Words so long buried inside he had no memory of where they had first been born.

"I gave my love a baby with no cryin'…" It was a mournful tune, unlike any music from Taos.

The song was a tunnel leading to someone he could barely remember.

"Bill-y," the memory of the vision echoed. "Bill-y."

The plaintive music continued: "How can there be a cherry without no stone?"

"When I was young like you…" Now it was Papá, that night. "…We crawled to the edge of the bluff and looked down."

"How can there be a chicken…"

"You are Soaring Eagle."

"…without no bone?"

"Let me finish, Son. This is important to you. It's where your silver coin came from…wagon…standing where it stopped, looking like nothing had happened…man and the woman…dead…little girl too."

"This isn't a vision," Julio cried aloud. "I'm

remembering! Remembering! I don't want to remember!"
But it was there, and he could not stop it. *We were sitting
by the trees. I didn't like Papá's story. It was making me
angry, and I wanted to ask him about me. I went for a
drink. Papá was whispering.* "There was a little boy, too,
a baby...skinny little thing, bundled in a blanket in that
blazing July heat." *JULY! That's why...*

"Julio means July!" Julio's eyes popped open. "It was
me! That baby was me! Papá was...That's why he called
me July!"

One last memory surged forward. "There's someone at
the fort now who may know who the people in the wagon
were."

The vision came that night.

It was the fort—Bent's Fort, sagging, in flames. Great
explosions shook the earth, dissolving Papá's hard adobes
into puffs of dust. Julio could see no people, only bursting
gunpowder and cannonballs, crumbling walls, and flames.
Billowing black smoke and dust, and the fort slowly, ever
so slowly, dying before his eyes.

On his return Julio expected to be greeted with honors.
Chivita would dash out ahead, then the elders would lead
a procession to meet him. Dancing Feather and Silent
Walker would be close behind. White Buffalo would be
standing back, waiting to interpret his vision.

"White Buffalo," Julio would say carefully in English, standing proud, "I have had a vision. I have eagle feathers to trade for a horse. I know who I am."

Crossing the river, he bathed away the dried blood, dirt, and sweat, glad the eagle's scrapes and pecks would not wash away. They were evidence of the battle, proof of his bravery.

As he came closer to the camp, Julio began to run. "My people!" He laughed. "Here I am!"

But as he rounded the last curve and darted through the cottonwood trees, he skidded to a stop and stared in disbelief. The tribe had moved on.

Chapter Twenty-Two

The whining came from near the river. Julio dropped the willow loop he'd found and ran. "Chivita?" he called. "Chivita!"

When Julio saw her, his temper flared. How could Silent Walker have left her like this? What if wolves or a bobcat had come along? The long buffalo-hide leash tied around her neck was entangled in tree roots and shrubs and the bundle Helacio had brought for Papá. Chivita could move only a short distance in any direction, not far enough to reach the gourds of meat and water. When she saw Julio, her whine broke into a happy bark.

"Chivita, hold still." She was trying to jump and lick and bark all at once. Julio slipped the knife under the leash, and she was freed. Fast as an arrow, Chivita shot into the cottonwoods, then rebounded, leaping on him, rushing to the water gourd, and back to Julio. "Where did they go, Little Goat?" Julio scratched behind her ears. "How long have they been gone?"

And why so suddenly? Why hadn't Dancing Feather waited for him? He would never have gone away without telling Dancing Feather. He didn't know if the pain in his chest came from running or from a feeling of betrayal.

"Come on, Chivita." He tied Papá's bundle onto his sash. "Let's go," he said, patting his thigh. "It's just the two of us again."

Julio stepped into a fast, even pace. The tribe had gone in a hurry and were moving toward the east. The horses' hoofprints gouged deep, much more deeply than when he had traveled with them, a sign they were being pushed. But why? Had they sighted more buffalo?

All the second day clouds gathered overhead, building toward a storm. Hoping for the comfort of a tipi, Julio had pressed on past a rock overhang and later a hollow tree where he could have kept dry. Now he and Chivita crested a sand hill, and there below sat the village. The tipis were in place; a fire roared in the fire circle. Familiar horses, decorated with paint, were tied head to head with horses Julio had never seen before. And the Cheyenne! They, too, were smeared with paint, whooping, galloping, and dancing around in the middle of the circle of tipis as if they were possessed.

Chivita strained forward and growled.

"No, Chivita. No." Julio scanned the gyrating mass of horses and people for Silent Walker or Dancing Feather but could see neither one. "They're getting ready for battle, Chivita. Or just returning." Julio eased down onto the ground beside her. "I've never seen them like this."

Julio spotted White Buffalo in a cluster of riders heading toward the village. White Buffalo sat forward on his horse, holding high a long spear. His face was painted black. Black, the color of victory. *So*, Julio thought, *the battle has already been fought.*

At a command White Buffalo and all the blackfaced riders raced into the village, shooting rifles, shouting, and waving spears. They circled and circled until finally, in the dust-filled clearing in front of the tipis, they stopped. White Buffalo spoke, gesturing with his hands, pointing with the spear, telling about the skirmish.

From what Julio could understand of the signs, they had ridden farther east along the Arkansas River and battled their old enemies, the Pawnee. They had captured horses. *Maybe mine!* Julio reached into his leather bag for the eagle feathers next to Teresita's stone. *If I could choose now, Teresita,* he thought, *I would take the white one with red-brown splashes of color. If I could choose another, I'd take the shining black one for you.*

The Cheyenne's initial frenzy fell into a rhythm as the drumming began. Women scurried into tipis with firewood, and soon small fires inside made the tipis glow. The smoke blended with the close, gray sky. Yelps and wails rose from within the encampment and echoed from the squat hills.

Julio's heart was beating too fast. He wanted to find Silent Walker and Dancing Feather, yet he was reluctant to walk into that melee. He had never seen the Cheyenne like this before. Once, he'd heard them, but that was before he could see and before he really knew them. They were so agitated, anything might happen. He decided to wait for them to calm down.

"It's good they've returned in victory," he said to Chivita. "But why do they fight?"

As the sky darkened, the fires below gleamed redder and hotter. The drumming continued, incessantly. Julio thought he had not been seen, but a horse and rider moved away from the wild dancing, zigzagging up the loose slope of the sandy hill. As he drew near, Julio recognized the silhouette. It was White Buffalo.

"Soaring Eagle," White Buffalo greeted Julio by his new name. "You have returned from your quest."

"I have." Julio's practiced speeches vanished.

White Buffalo rested one wrist over the other on his horse's mane and looked down over the celebrating village. "Nothing lives long," he said, "only the earth and the mountains."

Julio shivered. Those were Dancing Feather's words.

"There was a battle, Soaring Eagle." White Buffalo's voice was scratchy; he sounded old.

Julio couldn't breathe. Something had happened to Dancing Feather or Silent Walker. "What?" he asked, his voice a harsh whisper. "What happened?"

"Dancing Feather has followed the honorable path of the ancient Tse-tsėhésė warrior."

Everything stopped. Life, breathing, the stars, the drums. Everything. "But it was a victory!" Julio whirled dizzily to his feet. "You're wearing black paint! You won! How...?" He grabbed up Papá's bundle and ran.

A terrible scream traveled with him. Was his. "Dancing Feather! My brother! Noooooooo! You can't be dead! Not you too!" He tripped and fell on the ground, sobbing. "I must go to Silent Walker!"

White Buffalo's iron—strong grip closed around Julio's arm. "No," he said, leaning down from his horse. "Don't do it. It is better that you wait here until tomorrow."

Julio jerked away, running, stumbling down the sand hill, pushing, jostling his way through the gyrating mass around the fire. The hooves of White Buffalo's horse drummed behind him across the worn prairie grass and into the throbbing Cheyenne circle.

Silent Walker sat on the ground, thrashing like a mad animal, her face contorted, mouth opened in an inaudible scream. Blood streamed from her shredded face. Julio stared, aghast, as he felt White Buffalo's hand close around his arm. "What have they done to her?"

Silent Walker's silent screaming was more terrifying than the screeching of the other two women. Their cries rose and fell, horrible sounds, hateful, terrifying sounds, unimaginable sounds from women.

"They are crying for vengeance," White Buffalo said quietly. "It is the way of Tse-tsėhésė women."

"But who? Who did this to them?" Julio was ready to fight anyone—anyone!—who had.

"Soaring Eagle," White Buffalo said, "they've done it to themselves."

"Ay, Dios!"

Silent Walker snatched up the bloody knife from the ground before her, leapt to her feet, and drew it toward her face.

"No!" Julio grabbed her hand. "No! Silent Walker! No! Don't hurt yourself anymore. Please. No!" He wrestled with her, finally crushing her hand until the knife dropped. Her eyes glared hatred at him. Blood dripped from her chin and earlobe onto the white leather of her dress. With a mighty jerk she freed herself and lunged for the blade.

"Soaring Eagle, come away," White Buffalo said. "There is nothing you can do until this is finished. It is the Cheyenne way. Come."

Julio staggered back from Silent Walker, letting himself be led. *"It is the Cheyenne way."* How many more times would he hear those words?

"Ay, Dios!" Julio fell to his knees. "Help her! Oh, God, please, help her."

The angry sky darkened. Rolling gray clouds rumbled. Julio leapt to his feet, shaking his fists overhead. "I hope you have what you wanted now, Dancing Feather!" he yelled at the sky. "Your damned selfish death with honor! See? See what it has done to her?"

"Shhh! Shshhh!" Néške'e's arms were around him, holding him to her, rocking. "Shhh!" Chivita nuzzled against him, whimpering. Julio reached down and touched Chivita's head, then stumbled past the tipis and away from the fire circle just as the rain began.

Chapter Twenty-Three

"Nothing lives long, only the earth and the mountains." Like a rhythmic chant, the memory of Dancing Feather's prayer entwined with the beat of the drums.

"Nothing lives long"—*boom! boom-boom-boom*—"only the earth"—*boom! boom-boom-boom*—"and the mountains." Incessant, the "victory" drums sounded through the rain, hollow spirits flowing over sand hills.

Julio crouched outside the frenzied celebration, both arms pressed to his ears, grasping his fingers at the nape of his neck. He did not want to hear—either the drums or his thoughts.

Dancing Feather, dead. Stupidly, senselessly dead! Silent Walker, like Néške꞉e, scarred forever. *They're savages! Just savages!*

"It's our way Julio. It's the Cheyenne way. Nothing lives long..." *Boom! boom-boom-boom.* "You're making a mistake."

"Damn you, Dancing Feather!" Julio screamed. He jumped to his feet, shaking his fists at the dark sky.

The drums tugged at him, pounding his brain, intensifying each raw emotion. Even his breathing was drawn into the beat of the drum. In. *Boom!* Out. *Boom-boom-boom.* In. *Boom!* Out. *Boom-boom-boom.*

In spite of the rain a large fire cast its red glow and the distorted shadows of dancers up into the cottonwoods. Julio glared into the circle of tipis. A shriek rose above the drumbeat, then dived back into silence. He shuddered. *How could I have thought this might be my life?* The leather necklace snapped at his tug. He flung it at the gyrating shadows with a cry: "There is no Soaring Eagle, Dancing Feather! Not without you!"

"Come on, Chivita! We've got to get away from here!" Julio ran out into the darkness, his moccasins stepping high in the slick wet grass to avoid tripping over what his eyes could not see. Farther and farther to the east he fled, following the edge of the line of trees that bordered the river, until the pinging of raindrops on the cottonwood leaves and the lazy swishing of the Arkansas erased all but the nearly indistinguishable pulse of the victory dance.

Under the trees he felt for dry leaves and branches, then with sparks from his flints he built a fire. From the fire he lighted a torch. With it he could see. He chose a protected spot at the base of one of the old creaking cottonwoods to spread Papá's sarape. He placed the bundle of Papá's old clothes on it, then, one by one, each piece of his own clothing. "Chivita. Stay."

He walked out onto the plain, raindrops chill against his bare skin. Wet, the whole prairie smelled of sage, sweet and fresh, as if it were trying to help erase from his mind's eye the slashes on Silent Walker's face, the fact that Dancing Feather was gone. The sage tugged at him, and in spite of his anger Julio calmed. He knelt, listening. "Nothing lives long, only the earth and the mountains."

The torch hissed and flickered out, but in the darkness he felt the sagebrush. He broke off seven small branches. With each one he spoke in his heart to the bush, thanking it, feeling again the connection. "Ha ho," he said aloud after he had plucked the seventh.

It was then he felt the hand on his shoulder. "Ay!" he cried. He jumped to his feet and twisted around, the dark torch whizzing through the air like a weapon, but there was no one there.

"Santa María!" Tripping, staggering over clumps of sage and buffalo grass, Julio lunged toward the light of his fire.

He was shaking, but not from being cold. He piled more wood on the fire, scrambled into his clothes, and hugged

Chivita to his chest. *Someone* was here with him. He felt it in the back of his neck, prickling. Burying his head in Chivita's fur, he pressed his eyes closed, but the presence hovered even more closely. Chivita hummed, low. She broke free of his grasp and stared intently at a spot in the air where there was nothing.

"All right!" Julio finally cried out, looking up. "I'm not angry with you anymore!" He leapt to his feet. "You had your death with honor. That's what you wanted, isn't it? Not to die an old man?" He peered into the darkness, hoping not to see, fearing he would. "It's—" His throat tightened. "It's just hard for me to—" His breath caught. His hands tightened into fists. "But see what you've done to Silent Walker!" Then without warning his knees buckled and sank deep into the soggy prairie. A long, low wail came up from his throat, through his mouth, his lips. "Oh, Dancing Feather! I've lost you. I lost Papá, and now I've lost you too! "

The fire flared, and a charred leaf lifted up from the flames. Languidly it spiraled on the updraft, higher and higher, circling around and around and around, floating on air. Julio held his breath, watching. A gust of wind rustled the branches, and water sprinkled down from the trees, knocking the leaf back into the fire. In a puff it flared and was gone.

"Ha ho!" Julio whispered. "I will miss you, Dancing Feather."

Before he lay down to sleep, Julio knelt and prayed to every god he knew. He made the sign of the cross and rubbed Teresita's stone. He circled his bed with Chivita in their ancient ritual, missing the sheep, but the last prayer was to his mother, the mother who called him Billy. Dancing Feather had sent him a sign. Now he asked her for another.

Chapter Twenty-Four

Early the next morning Julio bathed in the river. His dreams had not brought a sign. Papá and Dancing Feather were dead. He pondered his vision of the crumbling fort and wondered how many more disasters lay ahead.

Julio flipped the river water from his hair, brushed it from his body, then paused over the bundle of Papá's old clothes. For what he was about to do he needed something clean.

His fingers worked slowly, as if reluctant to pry into secrets. The knots gave. Inside the outer wool shirt was another, more tattered; inside it a pair of trousers; and inside them worn sandals. Beneath the sandals he found a cloth-covered rectangle about the size of both his hands. The wrapping around it was new white cotton, a handkerchief for Papá he was certain Teresita's hands had spun and woven and hemmed.

He picked up the package and turned it over. As the cloth slipped away, a ray of sun flashed on gold. He wouldn't have been more startled to see a gold ingot in Papá's things, but this gold shone on the edges of the pages of a book. His fingers traced a symbol on the cover—*B*—that looked like a gold *1* and *3* pushed close together.

Inside, among the many pages of writing, were pictures of strange people and places and plants, highlighted with gold. Where had Papá gotten it? And *why?* Papá couldn't read. Julio had never seen any book in their house, or in the houses of any Montoyas. Only at the home of Father Martínez had he ever seen anything like this, but that book was much larger and bound in wood with metal hinges.

At one end of the book were pages with lines and spaces and what looked to him like handwritten signatures and dates joined together by lines. He could decipher only the dates 1829 and 1831.

1831. This was 1845. "Thirty-two, thirty-three, thirty-four..." He counted the years on his fingers. There were fourteen. That last night Papá had said, "When I was young like you, thirteen, fourteen years old..." Julio stared down at the lines and squiggles that were only mysteries to him. Never, not even at Papá's grave, had he yearned more desperately to know how to read and write. "Someday..." It was a promise he knew he would keep.

The wagon was standing, Papá said. It had not burned. The tiny silver coin came from there. Julio felt certain the book had come from the wagon too. Carefully he wrapped the book in the woolen shirts with the rest of his clothing and retied the cord around the bundle. He pulled on Papá's trousers, rolled the bottoms into cuffs, and fixed the sandals to his sash.

Returning to the river, he dampened the new white handkerchief and walked across the cool, washed plain, back into the continuing throb of drums. The morning felt fresh and new, not yet born. Clouds still lingered, leeching the earth of color.

Julio slipped into the Cheyenne circle. He found Dancing Feather's bear claw, scooped it from the ground, and made his way to Silent Walker's tipi.

It had been a long time since he'd played his flute, a long time since those simple days in the field with the sheep, but he reached into the leather bag. His fingers felt at home on the carved round holes, as if they'd never been away. When he blew, the air passed through the reed flute, and his tune was sweet, low, and mournful— the one he'd heard and remembered.

"How can there be a cherry without no stone?
How can there be a chicken without no bone?

How can there be a ring without no end?
How can there be a baby with no cryin'?"

A tiny rustle came from inside, and the buffalo-hide
flap opened a crack.

"Silent Walker, please, come out." His voice surprised
him. It was calm, deeper than it used to be.

Hesitantly Silent Walker crept from the tipi, covering
her face with outspread hands.

"Silent Walker," he said softly, "I'm sorry. I'm sorry
about Dancing Feather. We will both cry for him for a
long, long time." He said it in English and hoped she
could understand. Reaching out, he pulled her hands
away from her face. She ducked her head to the side,
trying to hide behind the tunnel of unbraided hair. Her
cuts were beginning to scab over. Dried blood was caked
on her skin and in flaking rivulets down her neck.

"Here," he said, holding her chin on his fingertips. As
gently as he could, he dabbed the damp handkerchief on
her face to clean away the stains. Silent Walker's eyes
closed, and beneath the lashes tears began to flow.

Julio reached again into his leather bag. "This is for
you." He took her hand and laid the eagle feathers across
her palm. "And this, to keep for me." He placed Dancing
Feather's bear claw necklace on top.

She looked up, this time, her eyes meeting his. She
pointed, first toward the east, then in a circle, indicating

the tipis, herself, Tse-tsėhėsė life.

"I don't know," he said, shaking his head. She nodded, leaving her head bowed.

Without looking back Julio turned and walked away. As he left the ring of tipis, a pebble thumped against the calf of his leg. He did not turn.

When he saw it, he felt little surprise, only an overriding sense of sadness. Bent's Fort looked exactly as it had first appeared in his vision, so huge it could hold all of Taos inside the buff-colored adobe walls Papá had helped make.

Awed by its grandeur, Julio let his eyes follow the tall, round bastions to a blaze of blooming cactus outlining the tops of the dirt-colored western walls. "Papá," he whispered, "you must have been very proud."

Helacio's sheep were grazing near the river. A small band of Kiowa approached from the north to trade. Clusters of men—American men—were whooping and yelling as two horses raced around an oval track west of the fort. Not far from them other men, using metal shovels with hardwood handles, were digging a grave in a dusty cemetery near the walls of the fort.

Around loaded wagons in front of the metal-clad gates wagon masters were crying "Ho!" and "Gee!" and "Haw!" as they guided lumbering oxen into place to be hitched.

With a start Julio noticed the flag flying from the belfry above the gates—red and white striped with stars on a blue corner. Stars. Dancing Feather's words echoed from the canyon: "When Bent's Fort was built, stars fell from the sky. The Tse-tsėhésė thought the world was dying."

Is the world, the fort, the Cheyenne nation dying, as Dancing Feather said, little by little like an old man? I don't know. I don't know what these signs and visions mean. I don't know where I belong, or what I will do.

From the rise on which he and Chivita stood, Julio could still see the gray silhouettes of the Cheyenne village and hear the hint of drums. Behind them, deep in the distance, hidden in clouds, were his mountains and Taos. Before him lay Bent's Fort and, stretching farther eastward, the plains and the ever—widening Santa Fe Trail, which led to Saint Louis and Independence and other places whose names he'd heard but could not remember.

He knelt beside Chivita, stroking her wiry hair. "I'm not Mexican, and yet I am. I'm not Cheyenne, and yet I am. But...what else am I?"

He scratched Chivita's ear. "Your mother wasn't really a goat; she was a dog, just like you. Somewhere there is someone like me too—a grandmother, maybe. An aunt, an uncle, a cousin. Someone with green eyes and straw-colored hair and a relative named Billy. I want to know who.

"Let's go, Chivita. At Bent's Fort, Papá said, there is someone who may know." Taking in a deep breath, Julio strode out onto the Santa Fe Trail, eastward bound, clasping the book to his side.

Author's Notes

The setting for *Soaring Eagle* came from my childhood in southeastern Colorado. Ideas came from adventures in that place—"my place"—exploring along the Arkansas River, searching in deep dry canyons for pictographs, petroglyphs, and pottery sherds, and standing awe-struck in the adobe ruins of Bent's Fort. Inspiration came from the ancient whispers of the people who walked this land before me.

To gain the historical background needed to write *Soaring Eagle*, I read books, journals, diaries, cookbooks; studied old maps; and found music, games, and stories of the era. I threw myself into experiential on-site research, doing what my characters would do, going where they went, facing the challenges they would face. I found where Julio's home would have been in Taos, followed his footsteps out of the Taos Valley, experienced too much exposure to sunlight on snow, participated in a sweat lodge, slept alone on the Trail, spent days (and nights) in the then reconstructed Bent's Fort, and encountered, up close, a porcupine outside my window, a coyote that ran across the foot of my sleeping bag, and a bear—a beautiful brown bear that glowed red as the sun set behind him.

Soaring Eagle is a work of historical fiction. The main characters were born in my imagination. Their lives move through actual places and events and interact with people who actually lived in the mid-1800s, the time of this story. *Soaring Eagle*, the first book in the Santa Fe Trail Trilogy, is followed by *White Grizzly* and *Meadow Lark*.

What's Fact? What's Fiction?

Julio, his family and friends—José, Dancing Feather, Silent Walker, Néške?e, and his dog Chivita—are fictional characters. What happens to Julio in the story—the plot—is fiction interwoven with fact and emotional truth.

Taos. Julio's home, the small village of Taos in northern Mexico is an actual place. Today, Taos is in New Mexico. Near the town of Taos, Pueblo Indians still live in the nearly thousand-year-old pre-Hispanic Taos Pueblo. In Julio's time, Jicarilla Apaches often raided crops and livestock in the Taos Valley. Fandangos, Taos Lightning, and church bells greeted new arrivals. Father Martínez was a politically active, party-loving priest of the Catholic Church. William Bent's brother, Charles, lived in Taos, as did Ceran St. Vrain. The three business partners, William Bent, Charles Bent and Ceran St. Vrain, built Bent's Fort as part of a large trading empire along the Santa Fe Trail. [For photos and further information on the ancient Taos Pueblo, see the National Park Service site http://nps.gov/history/worldheritage/taos.htm.]

The Santa Fe Trail. The Santa Fe Trail was the trade route between Santa Fe in northern Mexico and Missouri on the western border of the United States.

Beginning in 1821, when the first American traders reached Santa Fe, until 1880, when the Santa Fe Railroad reached Santa Fe, the Santa Fe Trail was a major artery between the east and the west. Traders, hunters, trappers, merchants, and, later, military troops and settlers traveled the Santa Fe Trail back and forth across the Plains Indian Territory between Independence, Missouri, and Santa Fe. The Trail divided at the Cimarron Crossing of the Arkansas River. The Mountain Branch followed the Arkansas River to Bent's Fort near the present-day town of La Junta, Colorado. The other branch, the Cimarron Cut-off, shortened the trip by several days, but crossed a desolate area with little water where many travelers perished.

Ruts from the heavy wagons that traveled the Santa Fe Trail are still visible in the prairie grass. Today, U.S. Highway 50 follows much of the old Trail.

Bent's Fort. Bent's Fort was the most important stop on the Santa Fe Trail. Built in 1833 on Plains Indian Territory in what is now Colorado, Bent's Fort sat just across the Arkansas River from Mexico. The United States border lay six to seven hundred miles to the east. Travelers in ox-drawn wagons spent fifty to sixty days or more on the Trail between Missouri and Bent's Fort. It took another month to reach Santa Fe.

The Cheyenne and other Native American tribes traded peacefully at Bent's Fort. William Bent's first, second, and third wives were Cheyenne, and his children were half-Cheyenne, half-Anglo. William's son, George Bent (1843-1918), was wounded by Colorado troops during the infamous Massacre at Sand Creek. Following that dishonorable attack, George Bent rejected his father's heritage and fought as a Cheyenne Dog Soldier in the ensuing Indian Wars against the White Man.

In 1849, Bent's Fort was destroyed. More than one hundred years later, in the late 1950s, it was reconstructed. Early pen and pencil sketches, written descriptions, and the remaining ruins of the original foundations provided the necessary information for the Fort to be rebuilt. Today, more than a hundred and sixty years after the heyday of the original Fort, the reconstructed Bent's Fort stands as a monument to those exciting sixteen years before it was destroyed. Now, visitors pass through the *zaguán* into the glare of the sunny courtyard, explore the many rooms, and chat with modern-day re-enactors of history: adobe makers, trappers, guides, and perhaps even with William Bent himself.

To learn more about Bent's Fort, how to visit Bent's Fort, and how to participate in programs offered, check this Internet site: www.nps.gov/beol.

The Mexican-American War. At the time of this story, 1845, the United States had elected a new president, James Knox Polk. President Polk looked westward with ambition to acquire more land for his country. He was an advocate of "Manifest Destiny," a belief that the American West was "destined" to belong to the United States in spite of the fact that for centuries the land had been home to Native American and later, to Spanish and Mexican people.

At the time of President Polk's election, Texas was not a part of the United States. The land had belonged to Mexico, but Americans settled there and in 1836 named the area the "Independent Republic of Texas." The Independent Republic of Texas antagonized Mexico by taking land and attacking Mexican wagon trains and settlements, some as far north as the village of Mora, which is now in New Mexico.

At the same time as the growing hostility between Texas and Mexico, the United States was becoming increasingly divided, North against South, over the issue of slavery. Pro-slavery states wanted Texas to become part of the Union as another pro-slavery state. Many Americans feared that if President Polk annexed Texas, the hostility between Mexico and the Independent Republic of Texas would carry over into the relationship between Mexico and the United States. That is exactly what happened. In 1845, the United States annexed Texas, and in the following year the Mexican-American War began.

Details. In addition to historical facts about the Santa Fe Trail, Bent's Fort, Texas, Mexico, and the United States, many details in *Soaring Eagle* are also factual. The story Papá tells Julio about the River of Souls Lost in Purgatory is a true story. A stream now called the Purgatory, and sometimes the Picketwire, is the site where early Spanish explorers died searching for *Quivara*, Coronado's lost cities of gold. Years later, their bones and armor were found.

The details of Julio's life in Taos, his journey along the Trail and with the Cheyenne — play, work, fishing, hunting, lodging, food, clothing, ceremonies, language, and other customs — are true to life. Botany, geography, animal behavior and habitat are also factual.

The sad song Papá sings on the trail is a translation of an old Mexican *canción*. The song Julio remembers his American mother singing is a traditional folk song.

On August 21, 1849, four years after the time of this story, Julio's vision of the destruction of Bent's Fort came true. Read what might have happened in *Little Fox's Secret: The Mystery of Bent's Fort* also by Mary Peace Finley.

Glossary

A*do*be: A mixture of clay, water and a binder such as straw, poured into molds and sun dried to make bricks for building.

Ale*grí*a: A plant with red flowers.

A*rro*yo: A ravine.

A*to*le: Cornmeal mush made from dried corn that is roasted and ground.

Bent's Fort: In the mid-1800s, a trading post on the Santa Fe Trail in Plains Indian Territory across the Arkansas River from northern Mexico. Bent's Fort is in present-day Colorado.

*Bu*rro: A small Mexican donkey.

Ciga*ri*llo: Spanish for "cigarette."

Chillblain: Painful inflammation on the hands or feet caused by exposure to cold and moisture, often causing skin to split open.

Chi*vi*ta: Spanish for "little goat."

Compa*ñe*ros: Friends, companions.

Contra*yer*ba: An herb.

Emoonae: Cheyenne for "beautiful."

E-peva?e: Cheyenne for "thank you."

Fan*dan*go: A dance.

Ha ho: Cheyenne expression of appreciation. Thank you.

*Hi*jo: Spanish for "son." (The H is silent.)

*Ju*lio : July, the seventh month of the year. Also a name.

*Me*cha: Spanish for "wick."

Me*ta*te: A stone bowl for holding dried corn to be ground with a stone grinder called a *mano*, Spanish for "hand."

Mo²óhtavė-hohpe: "Black soup"—the Cheyenne word for coffee.

Néške²e: Cheyenne for "grandmother."

No com*pren*do: Spanish for "I don't understand."

Osh*a*: An herb whose root is boiled for tea and to treat colds.

Quien es us*ted*?: Spanish for "Who are you?"

Re*boz*o: A shawl or scarf worn by women.

Sa*ra*pe: An open-sided cloak.

Snowblindness: A painful condition of the eyes caused by overexposure to the glare of sunlight on snow and resulting in dimmed sight or temporary blindness.

Som*bre*ro: A large-brimmed hat.

Taos Lightning: A strong fermented beverage brewed in Taos.

Travois: A sled used by Plains Indians made by stretching hide or leather between two poles and pulled by horses or dogs.

Tse-tsėhésė: Cheyenne word for "Cheyenne."

*Ul*tima: The final one, the last one.

Vé²ho²e: Cheyenne for "white man."

*Vi*gas: Wooden beams, often whole logs, used to support a roof.

Wolverine: A ferocious four-legged predator, a mammal no longer encountered in the Colorado Rocky Mountain area.

*Za*guán: A covered entryway.

Clues to Pronunciation

Cheyenne is traditionally a language that is spoken, not written. The Cheyenne words in *Soaring Eagle* come from primary sources—diaries, journals, and books— written and interpreted by English speaking travelers to the West in the mid-1800s, as well as from more recent sources, both oral and written. The mark that looks like a question mark without a dot (ʔ) indicates a throat sound as in "oh-oh!" A dot above a vowel means that sound and the one before it are whispered. When a vowel is doubled, the sound lasts twice as long as the single vowel. The *s* with a circumflex (ŝ) is pronounced *sh* as in "ship."

About the Author

Mary Peace Finley grew up along the Arkansas River near the site of Bent's Fort and the old Santa Fe Trail. She attended public schools in Fowler, Colorado, and is a graduate of the University of Denver. She has taught English as a foreign language in Latin America and the United States and teaches fiction writing classes and workshops. Her award-winning historical novels, *Soaring Eagle, White Grizzly,* and *Meadow Lark,* make up the Santa Fe Trail Trilogy. Other publications include *Little Fox's Secret—The Mystery of Bent's Fort, The Matchbox, Tiger Tales, Fireflies,* and *Fernitickles*; magazine articles, and television scripts for *Marty Stouffer's Wild America.* She lives in Colorado.

Author Visits

Find information on author talks, school visits, and writing workshops at http://marypeacefinley.com. To inquire about scheduling an event, e-mail MaryPeaceFinley@att.net with "Author Visit" in the subject line.

"From her Native American flute to the block of Chinese tea, Ms. Finley captivated and delighted our students with opportunities to interact with her and her hands-on display."
                    – Vicki Fuesz, Sterling Middle School, Sterling, CO

"Your visit was informative, enjoyable, memorable, and FUN! You are a wonderful role-model for the writers at St. Anne's. These 6th graders on the journey with *Soaring Eagle* will remember your visit for a lifetime. That makes me very happy! I salute your integrity, your wisdom and your passion for writing and look forward to more visits with you."
                    – Midge Kral, St. Anne's Episcopal School, Denver, CO

"Mary's interaction with my 8th graders was fun, educational, and inspiring. She made the time period and her experiences come alive!"
                    – Kay Van Wechel, Falcon Middle School,
                    Colorado Springs, CO

Praise For The Santa Fe Trail Trilogy

Soaring Eagle

"This fast-paced adventure novel set in the southwest during the mid-1800s is a coming-of-age story of epic proportions. Finley weaves a compelling story of the tension between the encroaching American settlers, the Mexican residents, and the indigenous Native American Peoples."

– School Library Journal

"A good story well told."

–Tony Hillerman

"*Soaring Eagle*, a fine adventure tale, full of action and suspense, marks the debut of a promising writer."

–Theodore Taylor

"This historical coming-of-age story will certainly appeal to young readers."

–Booklist

White Grizzly

"Disaster follows disaster in this wonderful, exciting tale created by a writer thoroughly versed in her material."

– David Lavender, historian and author
of *The Santa Fe Trail*

"This novel is for young adults, but it certainly can be enjoyed by anyone looking to be a part of a compelling and suspenseful journey through three cultures, made completely realistic by brilliant writing, true characters, and genuine situations."

– Bloomsbury Review